'I haven't got

She stepped forw... something caught ... ...e jolt made her head fly around apprehensively. It was a strange notion, but she half expected to see Lucinda Fitzgerald beside her, tugging at her sleeve, imploring her to come back.

'You've caught your blouse on the handle of the door,' Quinlan remarked.

Once freed, she took one step forward and Quinlan closed the door behind her.

He smiled. 'Step into my parlour.'

Dear Reader

Well, summer is almost upon us. Time to think about holidays, perhaps? Where to go? What to do? And how to get everything you own into one suitcase! Wherever you decide to go, don't forget to pack plenty of Mills & Boon novels. This month's selection includes such exotic locations as Andalucía, Brazil and the Aegean Islands, so you can enjoy lots of holiday romance even if you stay at home!

The Editor

Kathryn Ross was born in Zambia where her parents happened to live at that time. Educated in Ireland and England, she now lives in a village near Blackpool, Lancashire. Kathryn is a professional beauty therapist, but writing is her first love. As a child she wrote adventure stories and at thirteen was editor of her school magazine. Happily, ten writing years later DESIGNED WITH LOVE was accepted by Mills & Boon. A romantic Sagittarian, she loves travelling to exotic locations.

Recent titles by the same author:

TOTAL POSSESSION
SCENT OF BETRAYAL

DIVIDED BY LOVE

BY
KATHRYN ROSS

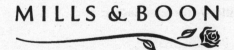

MILLS & BOON LIMITED
ETON HOUSE, 18-24 PARADISE ROAD
RICHMOND, SURREY TW9 1SR

All the characters in this book have no existence outside the imagination of the Author, and have no relation whatsoever to anyone bearing the same name or names. They are not even distantly inspired by any individual known or unknown to the Author, and all the incidents are pure invention.

All Rights Reserved. The text of this publication or any part thereof may not be reproduced or transmitted in any form or by any means, electronic or mechanical, including photocopying, recording, storage in an information retrieval system, or otherwise, without the written permission of the publisher.

This book is sold subject to the condition that it shall not, by way of trade or otherwise, be lent, resold, hired out or otherwise circulated without the prior consent of the publisher in any form of binding or cover other than that in which it is published and without a similar condition including this condition being imposed on the subsequent purchaser.

*First published in Great Britain 1994
by Mills & Boon Limited*

© Kathryn Ross 1994

*Australian copyright 1994
Philippine copyright 1994
This edition 1994*

ISBN 0 263 78507 6

*Set in Times Roman 10 on 11¼ pt.
01-9406-54697 C*

Made and printed in Great Britain

CHAPTER ONE

HOLLY pulled the chestnut mare to a halt at the top of the valley and leaned forward to pat her neck. Both horse and rider were out of breath from the long gallop over the lush green meadows, but both had enjoyed the exercise.

'Good girl, Becky,' Holly murmured in a low, soothing voice, and allowed the horse its head for a moment as it pulled idly at some grass beside them. The scent of horse-flesh mingled with the smell of new-mown grass in the warm evening air. Holly relaxed for a moment as her eyes swept over the rolling countryside.

She loved this place so much, she thought with a swell of pride as her eyes took in everything from the rolling Wicklow mountains around them to the softness of the green fields and the meandering river that flowed between them. Her beloved farm...she checked the thought immediately; the farm did not belong to her, it belonged to Flynn. Only Flynn didn't want the place any more, he wanted to make a new life for himself in Australia. Immediately the relaxed mood vanished, replaced by the tension that had gripped her over the last few months.

With a sigh Holly pulled at the horse's reins. There was no point thinking about her problems now; there were more practical things to see to. She needed to look at the fence further down the valley. One of the men had reported it was down when he'd passed earlier in the day. She urged the mare forward and they proceeded at a more leisurely pace.

She found the fence without any difficulty. It was down all right, and the damage was considerable, stretching along the southern perimeter of their land.

'Damn!' Holly leaned forward in her saddle, a look of dismay on her young face. The labourer who had reported the fence should have taken a few of the men and come down to see to this straight away. It was obvious that quite a few of their cattle had decided to make their way through to the next field. It wouldn't have been quite such a calamity if the next field hadn't belonged to their neighbour, Quinlan Montgomery.

Holly dismounted from her horse and went across to have a closer look.

A noise to her left made her head turn sharply and to her dismay she found herself looking directly into the laughing blue eyes of Quinlan himself.

He was standing on his side of the fence, long jean-clad legs slightly apart in an arrogant stance. 'Good evening, Holly.'

'Evening.' Her voice was curt, as it always was if she had to speak to him. She turned her attention back towards the fence, away from his disconcerting presence. Quinlan Montgomery was as handsome as the devil and twice as troublesome.

'I think the last time we met I did say that this fence should be electric.' His voice was drily amused.

'Did you?' Holly didn't look around. She knew damn well what he had said. She had known he was right at the time but she hadn't been able to afford the luxury of an electric fence—not that she would have told him that.

'Your cattle are down by my lake,' he said nonchalantly. 'One of them has bad cuts from the barbed wire. I think you'll have to call Ross Murphy out.'

Wonderful, Holly thought irately. Now, not only would she have the cost of repairing the fence, but a vet's bill as well.

'It would probably save you money in the long run to get the electric fence,' Quinlan continued as if reading her mind.

She turned sharp eyes on him. 'Thank you for the advice, Mr Montgomery,' she said with a note of disdain in her voice. 'But I really don't need it.'

'No?' His voice held blatant disbelief. 'What about my help rounding up your cattle—do you need that?'

'No, thanks.' For a fraction of a second she allowed her eyes to linger on him. He looked vital and strong, his energy and determination written in the powerful, perfect proportions of his body and the square line of his jaw. His thick hair was the colour of ebony and it gleamed healthily in the sunlight. His skin was tanned from the long summer days. Irritated by her interest in his looks, she gave a defiant toss of her long auburn curls and turned to mount her horse.

Quinlan watched her go, a thoughtful expression on his rugged features. She was an excellent horsewoman. Her slender body seemed to merge as one with the fluid movements of the horse as she urged her forward and across the fence down towards the lake.

She wore tight fawn-coloured jodhpurs and a plain black top that did little to hide the soft curves of her feminine form. Long auburn hair streamed behind her in wild disarray as she stood up in the saddle and leaned forward to whisper words of encouragement into Becky's ear. In a less experienced rider the movement would have looked clumsy, but Holly had been brought up in the saddle; she was at one with the animal beneath her and the rough terrain they were covering at high speed.

He turned away and made his way back to where he had parked his Range Rover. Holly was a true Fitzgerald:

proud, fiery and stubborn. It was a combination that had led to dramatic confrontations and disaster in the past.

Holly found the cattle without any difficulty and rounded them up with a skill born of years of practice to send them back towards her land. She drove them up a couple of fields so that she could have them safely enclosed behind a barred gate. Then she dismounted to examine the open gash on the side of one of the animals.

It was starting to get dark when she returned to the farmhouse. A thin wisp of smoke curled from the chimney into the purple velvet of the sky and a light shone from the open kitchen window. Flynn was home. Holly led Becky through to the stable and although she was tired she made sure she rubbed the animal down thoroughly and gave her fresh water before turning to go into the house.

The old farmhouse had a lot of character. Tangled creeper grew up the whitewashed walls and roses nodded around the doorway. In previous years it had been a very grand residence, but recently it had a neglected air about it. There was a lot of work needed to restore the place to its former glory. It needed a lot of time and a lot of money spending on it, and sadly they hadn't had much of either recently, Holly thought with a sigh as she crossed the cobbled courtyard to the front door.

Flynn was sitting at the kitchen table, his heavy boots resting on one of the pine kitchen chairs. 'Where have you been?' he demanded as soon as she entered the room. 'I'm starving!'

Holly resisted the temptation to ask why he hadn't cooked himself something instead of waiting for her. 'The fence is down on the border to the Montgomery land,' she said instead. 'I had to round up the cattle.' She crossed to the sink to wash her hands.

'I see.' Flynn's voice was flatly uninterested. 'What's for tea?'

'Vegetable casserole.' Holly crossed to the Rayburn. She had organised their evening meal early this morning, so hopefully it wouldn't be long.

'For heaven's sake, Hol... you know I like meat for tea.' Flynn scraped his chair back from the table, a look of impatience on his young face.

'I'm sorry, Flynn.' Holly's voice was gentle yet firm. 'But you know that I'm on an economy drive.'

The man raked a hand through his dark hair. 'You would think that one of the compensations for living on this God-forsaken farm would be an excess of meat,' he growled angrily.

Holly looked across at her young brother with a sadness in her dark sherry-brown eyes. 'Are you really so unhappy?' she asked softly.

'You know I am.' He turned away from her to stare out of the kitchen window. 'I feel trapped, Hol... my life isn't here. I haven't the heart to dedicate all my waking hours to the place the way you do. I want more.'

Holly bit down on the softness of her lip, her eyes studying the young man. In profile, Flynn Fitzgerald was very like their father: the same strong, tall build, dark, wild hair falling in an unruly way over his forehead, a determined look on the handsome features. Yet inside Flynn was completely different from Conrad Fitzgerald. Their father had loved this farm with a fierce passion, as had his father before him and so back through the generations. Flynn had no desire to work the land. His interests lay in other directions. He was a dreamer, with a strong artistic talent. The practicalities and rough manual work of a farm were not in his nature.

When their parents had been alive he had done his duty and worked alongside his father as had been expected of him. But since the tragic accident that had robbed them of both parents Flynn had gone more and more his own way. Now, like so many of the young people in the country, he wanted to leave Ireland and head for Australia.

Holly pushed a hand through her auburn curls in a tired, distracted way. She had some bad news for her brother and she had hoped to break it to him when he was in a better frame of mind. 'I had a letter from the bank this morning,' she told him gently.

He turned, a hopeful, questioning look in his eyes.

She shook her head. 'There's no way I'll be able to buy a half-share in the farm. The bank won't lend me the money.'

'Damn.' His voice was loud and filled with anger.

'I'm sorry.' She shrugged slim shoulders. 'If you will just give it some more time. Things are bound to get better soon and then, when we're showing bigger profits, the bank——'

'The bank can go to hell.' Flynn cut across her fiercely. 'I'll find someone else to solve the problem.' With that he turned towards the door and marched out into the night.

'Where are you going?' Holly ran after him, a note of panic in her voice.

'To the pub,' he muttered over his shoulder.

'But what about dinner?' Holly stopped short in the doorway. She was speaking to herself. Flynn was already climbing into his car.

She watched as he drove away, a feeling of helplessness creeping over her as the noise of the engine faded into the deep silence of the night. She turned and went back into the kitchen and sat for a moment at the table, her mind whirling in tired circles.

What on earth was she going to do? No answers sprang forward. It seemed her problems were insurmountable. She shook her head to rid herself of such a defeatist thought. She was a person who had a bright, optimistic attitude—she prided herself on being positive and practical; there was nothing she couldn't cope with. With that thought in her mind she stood up and went to ring the vet. After that, dinner was forgotten at the tempting thought of a hot, relaxing bath and the cool, scented sheets of her bed.

Sleep was evasive when she finally did crawl into her big double bed. Although her body ached with fatigue, she kept listening for the sound of Flynn returning. Poor Flynn, he had completely gone to pieces since the death of their parents. She knew in ordinary circumstances he would never leave her to run the farm on her own as he had been doing these last few months. No matter how he hated the place, he would be working alongside her each day until they got themselves together.

She closed her eyes and tried very hard to relax. Then, much to her consternation, she found herself thinking about Quinlan Montgomery. The darkness of his hair and those eyes, as vivid as the sea on a hot summer's day. She scrubbed the thought fiercely away. She disliked that man with every fibre of her soul.

The sound of a car made her scramble quickly out of her bed and reach for the white linen dressing-gown next to her. Thank heaven her brother was home safely. Maybe now they could sit and talk sensibly.

She hurried down the stairs and wrenched open the front door. 'Flynn, I'm so——' She broke off abruptly as she came face to face with Quinlan Montgomery for the second time that day.

Those deep blue eyes moved in an assessing way over her slender figure clad only in the revealing dressing-gown, her hair tossed in wild amber-red curls around the pale creamy skin.

'What are you doing here?' she demanded immediately, a furious hot wave of anger sweeping through her.

The last thing she wanted was a Montgomery setting foot on her land.

One eyebrow lifted sardonically. 'That's no way to greet a neighbour, Holly,' he chastised drily. 'Especially a neighbour on an errand of mercy.'

She stared at him blankly. 'What are you talking about?'

'Your brother.' He nodded back towards his car. 'I found him beside the road about a mile back.'

'Flynn!' Holly's skin blanched porcelain-white as she stepped forward into the darkness of the night, her heart thudding wildly against her breast. For a moment memories of her parents' accident surfaced with horrific clarity. She couldn't stand to lose Flynn the way she had lost them.

'It's all right, Holly.' Quinlan caught up with her and his arm went around her shoulder in an impulsive comforting gesture. 'There's nothing wrong with him that a good night's sleep won't cure.'

'Really?' She turned wide dark eyes up to him, her body trembling with reaction.

'Really.' He still held her and she knew he could feel how her body shook with fear. Abruptly she stepped back from him, taking deep breaths to steady herself.

He turned and opened the door of his Range Rover. Flynn was lying on the back seat fast asleep. Quinlan shook him roughly and he opened his eyes with bleary difficulty. For a moment he focused on Holly and smiled sheepishly. 'Sorry, Sis.' Then he passed out.

'If you hold the front door open I'll bring him in for you,' Quinlan said crisply.

She nodded and went to do as he asked.

It was a measure of how strong Quinlan was that he was able to lift the other man so effortlessly. Holly went ahead of him up the stairs and opened the door of Flynn's room for him. Her brother never stirred as the other man dumped him down without much attempt at gentleness.

Holly turned away and made her way back downstairs. She still hadn't pulled herself together. The aftermath of shock was making her legs feel like rubber. She went into the kitchen and poured herself a glass of water from the iced jug in the fridge.

'You could probably do with something stronger.' Quinlan's voice spoke from the doorway.

She shook her head. 'I don't drink.' She turned to look at him. He was leaning nonchalantly against the door-frame as if he were perfectly used to coming into this house.

In actual fact Quinlan had never been over the threshold. Her father would be appalled if he knew a Montgomery was in his house, she found herself thinking with a shiver of apprehension. She would have liked to order him out, except it seemed rude after his kindness in bringing her brother home. 'Would you like a drink?' she found herself asking instead.

One eyebrow rose in a mocking way. The offer obviously amused him but he nodded. 'Tea would be nice.'

Holly turned to fill the kettle. She had hoped he would have a cold drink, something he could toss back quickly before leaving. She set out a cup and saucer and then looked back at him. He was sitting at the kitchen table, watching her.

She pulled her dressing-gown tighter around her slender figure in an unconsciously protective way. His lips curved in a sardonic smile but he said nothing, just watched as she poured his drink and carried it over to him.

With an effort of will she forced herself to sit opposite.

'Well, now, this is cosy,' he murmured, the firm lips twisting in a half-smile. 'A Fitzgerald and a Montgomery taking tea together. Who would have thought it possible?'

Holly didn't care for his mocking tone. What he said was true. Her father would most certainly not have invited him to sit at their table. She felt an undercurrent of guilt mingling with uneasiness, but she swallowed down the feelings. 'Thank you for bringing Flynn home, Mr Montgomery.'

'Quin,' he corrected her automatically. His gaze wandered over the smooth paleness of her skin, the shadows under her large dark eyes. 'How are things going, Holly?' he asked suddenly. 'Are you managing?'

The question startled her. 'Of course we're managing.' She tilted her chin up defiantly. Quinlan was the last person to whom she would admit she was having problems.

He shrugged. 'I have noticed a deterioration in certain aspects of the farm. I just wondered if you need any help.'

'Certainly not.' Her voice rose sharply.

'Meaning that you would never accept help from a Montgomery,' he said drily.

'Meaning that I have everything under control,' she snapped firmly.

'If you say so.' He drank his tea and silence descended on them for a moment.

'Did Flynn leave his car on the road back there?' she asked him suddenly.

He shook his head. 'I'd say he left it in the car park at the pub and decided to walk home. He may be foolish but at least he had enough sense not to drink and drive.'

Holly glared at him. 'My brother is not foolish,' she told him angrily. 'It's just that he's had a lot on his mind recently.'

'Haven't we all?' Quin agreed drolly. 'But that isn't any reason for giving up on work, for getting blind drunk and worrying your sister half to death. Flynn needs to pull himself together.'

'And you need to mind your own business,' Holly told him furiously as she pushed her chair back from the table.

He shrugged. 'I'm only speaking the truth.'

'What would you know about our lives here?' she demanded crisply. 'You don't know the first thing about Flynn. He's a good, kind man——'

'So good and kind that he's leaving the complete running of the farm to you,' Quin finished drily.

'I don't have to listen to this.' Holly stood up.

Quin looked up at her with a gleam of amusement in his blue eyes. 'I take it the truce is over?' he enquired sardonically.

'I'm very grateful to you for bringing Flynn home.' Her eyes glowed with dislike as they rested on his attractive features. 'But I would like you to leave now.'

Much to her consternation, he laughed at that. It was a deep, rich sound in the silence. 'You don't believe in giving a guy a gentle hint, do you?'

She shrugged. 'I don't see any point in pretending. You know that there's no love lost between our families and you know why. I really don't want you on my property; I don't want you telling me how bad my brother is. Because, let's face it, he's a saint compared with the Montgomery family.'

'Sainted, is he?' Quin nodded sagely. 'Like the other members of the Fitzgerald family back through the ages,' he said humorously, then he shook his head. 'For heaven's sake, Holly, don't you think it's about time the past was forgotten?'

'If everyone forgot the past, how would anyone learn by their mistakes?' she ground out sardonically.

The amusement returned to his dark features. 'You aren't thinking of repeating your great-great-aunt Lucinda's mistakes, are you?'

'Don't be ridiculous!' She spluttered out the words, her face growing hot at the implications in that question.

'Well, that's all right, then.' For a moment his gaze raked over the slender lines of her figure, the heightened colour of her creamy complexion, then he scraped his chair back and stood up. 'Anyway, you needn't worry. I'm no Darcy Montgomery; I have no intention of seducing you,' he said lazily.

How dared he make such an outrageous statement? Holly's eyes blazed with fury and for a moment she was so intensely angry that she couldn't find her voice to answer him.

'You look upset,' he remarked with a gleam of humour. 'I hope I haven't disappointed you.'

'Disappointed me!' That riled her so much that she practically spat the words at him. 'I'd rather be seduced by a wild boar than by a man like you,' she finished contemptuously.

To her annoyance he seemed to find that most amusing. 'Well, there speaks a true farmer.' He laughed. 'A love for the livestock precedes everything else.' He glanced at his watch. 'On that amusing note I'd better go. I have a busy schedule tomorrow.' He glanced back at her. 'Would you like me to pick up Flynn's car for him tomorrow?'

The question startled her, coming so soon after the heated exchange. 'No.' She lifted her head to meet his eyes. 'We'll manage...thank you.' There was a note of stubborn pride in her voice and in the tilt of her head.

The firm lips twisted. 'A word of warning, Holly. I make a better friend than enemy.' With that he turned and made his way out into the hall towards the front door.

Holly followed at a safe distance. She could hardly wait to get him out of her house.

'Goodnight, Mr Montgomery,' she grated as he opened the front door.

'Goodnight, Ms Fitzgerald.' He turned to look at her, those blue eyes mocking. 'Or perhaps I should just call you Lucinda.'

Holly glared at him as he marched with that arrogant stride out towards his Range Rover. 'I suppose he thinks that's funny,' she murmured to herself as she slammed the door behind him. Damned infuriating man. She hoped it would be a long time before she set eyes on him again.

She locked the door and turned to switch the lights off, and, as she did, her gaze caught on the portrait which hung above the fireplace in the lounge. Lucinda Fitzgerald stared back at her.

It was a beautiful oil painting of the young woman at about the age of eighteen. Her red hair tumbled around her shoulders in a riot of long curls. Her eyes were wide and held a laughing glint that told of a love for life. She wore a deep green gown that was pinched in at the tiny waist and billowed around her feet. The resemblance between Holly and the girl was startling; it had been remarked on by many people over the years.

Holly flicked the light off and marched upstairs. Poor Lucinda's life had been tragically ruined by Darcy Montgomery. The Fitzgerald family would never forgive them... never.

CHAPTER TWO

IT FELT like the middle of the night when the alarm clock went off. Holly groaned and buried her head in the softness of her pillow. She had hardly slept at all last night and when at last she had dozed off her dreams had been plagued by Quinlan Montgomery, and the laughing face of Lucinda Fitzgerald.

With a sigh she reached out a hand and flicked off the alarm then she pulled the bedclothes back and got up.

Flynn was still asleep, she noticed as she passed his room. Judging by the state he had been in last night, she would probably not see him until later this afternoon. Holly went into the bathroom and turned on the shower. She had a million and one things to see to today and there was no time to worry about Flynn.

Dawn was creeping over the fields as she stepped out into the freshness of the early morning. She had always loved this time of day. As a child she had accompanied her father on his first round of the farm before she left to catch the bus to school. For a moment she thought longingly of those carefree days, riding next to her father, the only sound the early morning bird chorus and the occasional low moo of the cows. Then by contrast she found herself thinking of the life she had left only six months ago in Dublin.

At the age of eighteen Holly had got herself a very good job in Dublin. Then after a while the constant travelling in and out from the city had grown too much for her and she had decided to get a flat there. It had been a terrible wrench to leave her beloved home, but it was the sensible thing to do.

Her parents had been all for her moving; after all, the farm would one day be Flynn's and it was best that she start to make her own life, meet 'eligible young men', as her mother had put it.

Although there had been no serious men in her life, Holly had settled into a reasonably happy life in Dublin. She had found her job as secretary in a busy solicitor's office very enjoyable and her social life was good. Then, in the midst of her ordinary everyday life, tragedy had struck. Her parents had been killed outright in a horrific car accident and Flynn had gone completely to pieces.

When the telephone call had come Holly had been sitting at her office desk planning out her week's work. She had never got to do that work. The call had heralded a sudden vicious change in her life. Her parents were dead and Flynn needed her at home.

For a moment Holly's lips curved in a sad smile. Life never ran straight and true the way you expected. She had always known that Flynn would one day inherit the farm, but she had never thought that it would happen so soon... so tragically. She had never thought that she would be living back at home, to all intents and purposes running the farm. When Flynn had asked her to give up her job and come back to help him, she hadn't hesitated. She loved her brother and she would always be there for him.

As she looked about her now, at the beauty of the morning, she knew that she had made the right decision. This was her home, this was truly where her heart lay. The sun was coming up in a fiery red ball, dispelling the rolling mists of early morning, when she headed back towards the farmhouse again, her first tasks of the day over.

Ross Murphy's Land Rover pulled into the yard just as she slipped from Becky's back and she went across to greet him.

'Morning, Ross.' She smiled warmly at the vet.

'And a fine morning it is too.' He slammed the door of his vehicle shut and walked across towards her. He was a tall, thin man of about thirty, not handsome, yet there was something attractive about the good-natured grin on his face and the thick, unruly blond hair. 'Any chance of a cup of tea before I go up to see to your wayward cattle?' he asked, placing an affectionate arm around her shoulder.

'I suppose so,' Holly muttered, a teasing light in her dark eyes. 'And I suppose you'll be wanting something to eat as well?'

'I wouldn't say no.' He laughed.

'I thought not.' Holly shook her head in a despairing manner, but she was only joking. She had gone to school with Ross's sister Sinead, so she knew him well. They had always enjoyed an easy camaraderie, and she liked and respected him.

'How is Sinead?' she asked now as she led the way through into the house.

'Busy gallivanting and socialising.' He grinned. 'In about that order. She doesn't have any right to have such a successful business.'

Holly smiled. She was very fond of Ross's beautiful and vivacious sister.

'More to the point, how is Flynn?' he asked in a more serious tone.

Holly grimaced. 'Not good.' She finished putting some rashers of bacon under the grill and turned to look at him. 'He came home drunk last night.'

Ross shook his head. 'I know he's still in shock and it is only six months since the death of your parents, but he's going to have to pull himself together, for your sake as well as the farm's. Is he still going on about emigrating?'

Holly nodded. 'I had to tell him last night that I can't afford to buy a share in the farm. The bank won't lend me the money, not with the way things are at the moment.'

'So he marched off to the pub,' Ross muttered angrily. 'Does he realise the pressure he's putting on you?'

'Oh, I'm all right,' Holly dismissed airily.

Ross shook his head. 'You are not all right, Holly. For a start you're twenty-five years of age and I don't think you've had a night out in the last six months since the accident. Added to that, you're working from dawn to dusk and you look worn out.'

'I enjoy working on the farm,' she maintained stubbornly.

The smell of sizzling rashers started to filter through the kitchen and she turned to slice some fresh bread and make the tea. 'You'll never guess who brought Flynn home last night.' Deliberately she changed the subject. 'Quin Montgomery.'

A stunned silence met this remark for a moment. 'Don't tell me you allowed him into the house?'

'Well, I could hardly refuse, as he was carrying my brother at the time.' Holly grinned and brought the food over to the table to sit opposite him.

'Heavens above! I can hardly believe it!' Ross murmured. 'All these years of skirting around the Montgomery household and trying your best to avoid them and then you invite him into the house.'

Holly laughed. 'It was hardly a social occasion.'

'All the same, I'm very pleased.' Ross sipped his tea thoughtfully. 'It's about time the past was forgotten.'

'I didn't say anything was forgotten,' she told him hastily. 'I still don't like the man.'

Ross looked at her over the rim of his cup. 'Sinead thinks he's the most wonderful creature ever to walk God's earth.'

'That's because he's good-looking.' Holly wrinkled her nose. 'But underneath those good looks he's a shallow, horrid person.'

'I don't like to argue with you, Holly, but Quin is anything but shallow. He happens to be a very decent fellow, as most of the farmers around here will tell you.'

'Yes, well.' Holly sniffed in a dismissive manner. 'They would have to say that, as Quin happens to own nearly all the land around here and they're his tenants.'

'You're wrong,' Ross maintained firmly. 'I know you have your reasons for wanting to believe otherwise but I can assure you that everyone likes and deeply respects Quin.'

Holly finished her tea. 'Let's not talk about Quinlan any more,' she said briskly. 'The man irritates me.'

'OK.' Ross laughed and shrugged his shoulders. 'Lord Ashling is throwing his usual summer ball next week. Would you like to come?'

'I don't think I can, Ross——'

'Nonsense. You need to get out.' Ross grinned at her. 'And I'm not going to take no for an answer. I'll tell you what—we'll make it a foursome, drag Sinead and Flynn with us.' He sat back in his chair, looking very pleased at the idea.

'I don't think Flynn will go,' Holly said doubtfully.

'Leave him to me.' Ross pushed his empty plate away from him with a decisive hand.

Holly smiled. 'Well, if you can get Flynn to go, then you've got a deal.'

'We have a date, then. And now I had better get on with my work.'

'I'll come up to the field with you.' Holly stood up and cleared the table quickly.

As they walked outside Holly spotted one of her labourers, Nigel McGee, coming in through the yard gate. It was Nigel who had told her a fence was down yesterday and she called him over now to speak to him about it.

'You didn't tell me that it was our boundary fence with the Montgomery land that was down,' she said after the usual pleasantries of the day had been exchanged.

The man shrugged and looked completely unconcerned.

'Perhaps you would go up there now and repair the damage?' Holly asked briskly.

He nodded and walked away as if he had all the time in the world.

Holly turned exasperated eyes on to Ross. 'I don't know what on earth is wrong with the men. They all seem to be so slapdash these days. That fence would never have been left like that in my father's day.'

Ross nodded his head drily. 'If you want my opinion, I'd say they don't like taking orders from a woman.'

'But that's totally ridiculous!' she exploded furiously.

Ross shrugged. 'Yes, but that's the way they are. If Flynn were to show his face around a bit more, you might not have the same problem.'

Holly climbed into the passenger side of his Land Rover, an angry light in her face. She was damned if she was going to allow the men to get away with that kind of an attitude.

She simmered over the problem all the way up to the top field. Ross glanced at her sympathetically from time to time but said nothing until he pulled the Land Rover to a halt.

'Looks as if I was wrong.' He nodded his head over towards some workmen who were already mending the fence and grinned. 'You were worrying unnecessarily.'

Holly frowned and followed his gaze. Sure enough, there were several men working hard at the fence. But they were not her workmen and it looked as if they were fitting an electric fence, not mending the old one. She shot out of the Land Rover and marched down towards them, a determined look in her dark eyes.

'What's going on here?' She spoke to the man nearest to her.

He looked up for a fraction of a second then carried on working. 'Orders from Quin,' he muttered, as if that explained everything and no one would ever dare question Quin's orders.

This attitude just finished Holly's temper completely. 'Well, you can just stop what you are doing right now,' she ordered crisply. 'This is my fence and Quinlan Montgomery has no right to do anything to it.'

The man looked up at her for a moment. 'With respect, Holly,' he muttered, 'Quin has told us to do a job of work and we will continue to do it until he tells us to stop.'

Holly felt her blood-pressure soar. How dared this man ignore her instructions? How dared Quin Montgomery start interfering with her property?

'If you want to go and speak to Quinlan about it, one of the men is going up there now; you can ride up with him,' the man said now.

'Right, I will.' Holly turned to shout to Ross that she was going across to the Montgomery house and then with a militant stride she crossed over to her neighbour's property.

The young man who drove her up to the house didn't say much. One glance at Holly's furious face and he shut up after wishing her good morning.

Holly was seething. It was a combination of a lack of sleep, irritation with her own workers and the arrogant gall of Quin Montgomery. She supposed that his next move would be to send her a bill for the fence, and it would be a bill she would have difficulty in paying. Well, she would tell that arrogant, irritating man a thing or two.

The difference between the Montgomery land and the Fitzgerald was startling. This was a very well tended farm. Money was obviously no object. The house, when it came into view, took Holly's breath away. She had seen it before from a distance but she had never been this close to it.

Montgomery House was a fine Georgian residence. The building was three storeys high and more like a mansion than a farmhouse. It occupied an enviable position at the base of the valley, with sweeping views across well manicured lawns towards the countryside.

Holly went up the steps to the front door and lifted the heavy brass knocker to let it thud against the rich red door.

She had expected a housekeeper to answer the door, so she was taken aback when Quin opened it himself.

He was wearing jeans and a white shirt that contrasted sharply with his tanned skin and dark hair. There was no expression of surprise on the handsome features; he merely looked amused to see her.

'Well, now,' he drawled huskily. 'A Fitzgerald has come to call... how nice.'

'Don't get smart with me, Quinlan,' she flared up instantly, his sarcastic remarks like a whiplash across raw skin. 'What the hell do you think you're playing at?'

One dark eyebrow lifted in that expression she was learning to expect from him. He always seemed to find her entertaining; there was a gleam of laughter in the blue eyes that tormented her beyond belief. 'I haven't had a chance to play at anything yet this morning,' he said drily. 'I've been too busy working. However, if you would like to come back this afternoon, I might be able to come out to play then.'

Holly scowled at him. Her dark eyes would have burned a man less self-assured within forty paces. Quinlan was unmoved.

'You are interfering with my boundary fence,' she snapped, almost beside herself now with anger.

His lips twitched and she had the terrible feeling that he was going to laugh outright. 'Really... I had no idea it was that serious!' His shocked tone was laced with mockery.

'For heaven's sake, Quinlan,' she burst out furiously. 'I'm serious. I want to know why you've taken it upon yourself not only to mend my fence but to change it to an electric one.'

He stood back from the door. 'As you seem to be as charged up as the fence, I reckon you'd better come in.'

Holly hesitated. For years her family had deliberately kept their distance from this place. Now, less than twenty-four hours after Quinlan's taking tea in her kitchen, she was about to enter his domain. It felt ominously wrong. She had a crazy notion that the ghosts of Fitzgeralds back through the ages were at her elbow whispering warnings to her not to set foot inside this house.

'Well, I haven't got all day, Holly,' he grated impatiently. 'Do you want to discuss the damn fence or not?'

She stepped forward and as she did so something caught on her sleeve. The jolt made her head fly around apprehensively. It was a strange notion, but she half expected to see Lucinda Fitzgerald beside her, tugging at her sleeve, imploring her to come back.

'You've caught your blouse on the handle of the door,' Quinlan remarked, stretching out a hand to unhook the delicate crocheted material of her top.

Once freed, she took one step forward and Quinlan closed the door behind her. The noise of it slamming seemed to vibrate through her. She had the awful sense of starting something she was going to regret. She glanced up at Quin, apprehension clear in her wide dark eyes.

He smiled. 'Step into my parlour,' he invited mockingly as he waved a hand towards a door to her left.

She tossed her red hair in a defiant manner as she shook away the ridiculous thoughts. Of course she wasn't starting anything; she was just here to lodge a complaint.

The magnificent hallway with its sweeping staircase led into an equally beautiful drawing-room, pale yellow carpets with just a twist of turquoise to pattern the very centre of the room. Two settees facing each other across an Adam fireplace were in the same delicate shade of yellow, turquoise cushions echoing the pattern of the carpet.

'I'll get Mary to bring us some tea,' Quin said, and turned and left her before she could tell him she didn't want anything.

Holly bit down on her lip. This was totally ridiculous. She had come to do battle and he was turning it into a tea party. She stood at the windows and looked out over the green rolling countryside. Her temper seemed to have subsided as quickly as it had risen, which was rather typical of her. Now she just felt uncomfortable.

'Hello.' The young voice coming from just beside her made her jump violently.

'Sorry, did I startle you?' A little head peered out at her from behind the heavy tapestry curtain. 'I was hiding from Dad.'

'I don't blame you.' Despite everything Holly found herself smiling. There was no mistaking this boy for anyone other than Quin's son. He was only about five years of age and he had raven-dark hair and vivid blue eyes that shone with mischief.

Those eyes widened now and he grinned at her. 'Don't you?'

She shook her head. 'Not a bit. Between you and me, I feel like hiding from him myself.'

'Really?' The child regarded her seriously. 'There's room behind the other curtain if you want. I won't say anything.'

Holly laughed. It was a delightful sound in the silence of the room and she felt the tension that had invaded her body since last night disappear as if by magic.

'What's so funny?' Quinlan's voice interrupted the peal of laughter and she turned to look at him, her eyes dancing with merriment.

Holly was a beautiful woman, but when she smiled her face was transformed by a startling radiancy that seemed to emanate through the fine porcelain skin and the burnished glow of her long hair.

'Nothing, really.' She wasn't about to tell him that she had been considering hiding away from his disturbing presence.

For a moment he didn't say anything, just stared at her in a rather strange fashion. Holly's amusement faded and she stepped forward. 'So, Quinlan, perhaps you would like to explain to me about the fence.' She darted a glance back at the curtains and saw that the child had quickly hidden himself again.

He smiled. 'Certainly.' He waved her towards the settee. 'Make yourself at home.'

She frowned at that statement and the strange undercurrent she could sense in his voice. 'No, thank you.' Her dark eyes didn't waver from his. 'I'd rather stand.'

He shrugged. 'As you please.' Then suddenly he lifted his voice in a stern manner. 'Jamie, if you are not out from behind that curtain and back to your homework in two seconds flat there will be no barbecue for you tomorrow.'

There was a movement from behind the curtain again and the little boy came out, a rueful expression on his little face. 'Ah, Dad!'

'Never mind "Ah, Dad".' Quin pointed to the door. 'Back to your work.'

'Yes, Dad.' The child crossed the room dutifully. He was wearing a pair of white shorts that were a fraction too long on his chubby legs and a cornflower-blue top that exactly matched his beautiful eyes.

As she watched him Holly felt the strangest sensation of wanting to go across to him and pick him up. There was something about the child that made her heart go out to him.

'He's a holy terror,' Quinlan murmured drily, as the door closed behind him.

'Like his father?' Holly couldn't resist the gibe.

To her surprise Quinlan merely smiled and agreed. 'You're probably right.'

A young girl came into the room with a tray. She looked over at Holly with surprise. 'Hello, Holly!'

'Mary.' Holly nodded as she recognised the girl. Mary had worked in a shop in Greystones village before taking the job at Montgomery House.

'Fancy seeing you up here.' The girl placed the tray down on the polished rosewood table and left them.

Quin looked over at Holly, one eyebrow raised. 'You do realise it will be all over Greystones tomorrow that the rift between the Montgomery family and the Fitzgeralds has been healed and that we're having a torrid affair?' he said sardonically.

'Don't be ridiculous,' Holly snapped immediately. 'Mary wouldn't think anything like that. She was just surprised to see me in here.'

'And she will put two and two together and come up with six.' Quinlan grinned as Holly's skin started to glow with heat. 'You're easy to wind up, do you know that?' he added softly.

Holly clicked her tongue with irritation. 'When you have quite finished, Quinlan.' Her voice was sharply disapproving. 'I've come to discuss the matter of my fence.'

'Ah, yes, the fence.' He smiled and crossed towards the tray to pour two cups of tea. 'One lump or two?' he asked as he poised with one hand over the sugar.

'I don't want any damned tea,' Holly grated, her patience snapping. It seemed that Quinlan was deriving a great deal of pleasure out of goading her. In fact she was starting to wonder if the man had deliberately set his men to work on her fence knowing how it would annoy her. 'Look,' she burst out impulsively, 'just send me the damned bill for the fence and keep your damned nose out of my business in future.'

'If that's what you want.' He lifted the delicate china cup to his lips and took a sip of the brew. 'But I hadn't planned on charging you for the fence,' he said calmly.

Holly stared at him in disbelief. 'Since when has a Montgomery decided to do anyone such a favour...least of all a Fitzgerald?' she said scornfully.

'Since this morning.' He remained perfectly calm.

What would it take to rile that smooth, irritating manner? she wondered angrily. She would have loved to possess the answer. It would have given her no end of pleasure to raise his blood-pressure and annoy him the way he was annoying her. 'I don't need your patronage, thank you,' she told him crisply. 'I'm not that desperate.' With that she turned and headed towards the door. 'Just send the bill.' Then she marched out with her head high.

It was only when she stood outside on the doorstep that she realised she was going to have to walk home and it would take a good hour from here.

'Damn!' Her voice sounded loud in the silence of the morning. She had a million jobs to see to today; wasting time walking would mean she would finish very late again.

The door opened behind her. 'Having problems?' Quinlan enquired laconically.

'No.' Holly didn't look around at him. If he was laughing at her it would set her temper soaring again.

'If you want to hang on for a few minutes I'll drop you home,' he offered smoothly.

'Thanks—I'd rather walk.' She set off at a brisk pace down the driveway.

Holly wished she were wearing something a little cooler than the crocheted top and beige jodhpurs. The haze of early morning had lifted and the sun was blazing down unmercifully on the tarmac. She had been walking for about twenty minutes and still hadn't reached the end of the drive. The sound of a car engine broke the peaceful drone of the bees in the well stocked flower borders beside her and she glanced around as Quin drove by in his red Lotus.

'Damn man,' she muttered.

As if he had heard her, the car came to an abrupt halt a few feet away in front of her. She continued to walk at the same pace, intent on ignoring him.

'Would you like that ride now?' The passenger door swung open against a bank of foxgloves and red roses, effectively blocking her path.

She glared in at him.

'Come on, Holly, you're being daft,' he said calmly. 'I'm passing the end of your drive anyway and I'm sure you have a lot of work you want to be getting on with.'

Holly hesitated, then, swallowing her pride, she climbed into the luxurious leather seat next to him. 'Thanks,' she muttered drily.

'You're welcome.' The powerful car pulled away smoothly and they didn't speak until they reached the gates to his property and were out on the road.

'Jamie thinks you're very pretty.'

The comment startled her and she just shrugged. 'He seems a nice little boy.'

'Despite his wicked father?' Quin enquired drily, then went on to ask briskly, 'He wants to know if you would like to come to his birthday party tomorrow. He's having a barbecue.'

Holly turned surprised eyes on to him. What on earth was Quinlan up to? First that most peculiar offer to pay for her fence, now an invitation to his son's party... it was most disconcerting. 'Thank you, but I can't spare any time these days,' she muttered in a low tone.

Quin made no attempt to try to change her mind. 'I know you have a lot of work on now at the farm. I was sorry to hear about your parents, Holly,' he added softly.

She let the remark pass in silence. Apart from the fact that her loss was still raw inside her, she didn't want to discuss her parents with him.

'Jamie will be disappointed,' Quin continued briskly. 'For some reason he seemed to take to you.'

They pulled in through the gates to her property.

'You can leave me here,' Holly told him hastily.

'I may as well drop you at the door.' He made no attempt to slow the car until the farmhouse came into sight.

'Thank you,' Holly said awkwardly as he pulled to a halt right at the front door.

'You're welcome.' The firm lips twisted into an attractive smile as he watched her climb out.

'Don't forget to send me that bill for——'

The red Lotus pulled away, cutting her off in midsentence. 'Charming!' Holly muttered with a shake of her head as she watched him speed away.

'Was that Quinlan Montgomery?' Flynn hurried out through the front door.

'Yes, it was.' Holly turned accusing eyes on to her brother. 'The same Quinlan Montgomery who carried you home last night.'

Flynn looked sheepish for a moment, then grinned. 'Well, at least I had the excuse of alcohol. What's your excuse?'

'A broken fence.' Holly turned to go into the house. 'You don't think I would have anything to do with a Montgomery, do you? I remember what Dad said about them far too clearly.'

Flynn followed her. 'I think Dad went on a bit too much about that family sometimes,' he murmured thoughtfully. 'After all, there's only Quinlan left of them now, and he has never done anything against us.'

'You're just salving your conscience because you allowed him to bring you home last night,' Holly said firmly. 'If Dad were alive he would have had apoplexy.'

'Maybe.' Flynn shrugged. 'But the fact is that Montgomery stopped to pick me up from beside the road last night. I think that was quite decent; he could have driven straight past me.'

'Yes, it's hard to work out,' Holly murmured thoughtfully. There was definitely something weird going on. Why should Quinlan start playing at being the good neighbour when they had ignored each other for years? There was Flynn last night, the fence this morning...the lift and invitation to his son's birthday party! Holly felt very uneasy as she thought it over. She didn't trust that man; she didn't trust him at all.

CHAPTER THREE

'YOU look fabulous!' Sinead stepped back and admired her friend with great enthusiasm. 'More like the old Holly.'

Holly's eyes moved over her reflection in the bedroom mirror. She hardly recognised herself. For the last six months since she had come back to the farm she had been wearing nothing but jeans or jodhpurs. Now she stood resplendent in a long blue silk gown. It fitted the slender contours of her body perfectly, showing a creamy expanse of bare shoulders and dipped between her breasts in an extravagant swirl. Her hair had been swept upwards and only a few long amber curls were left to twirl tantalisingly down her long neck.

'It's a beautiful dress,' she murmured, feeling guilty all over again as she remembered how much it had cost to hire.

'You're only young once,' Sinead said firmly as she correctly interpreted her friend's thoughts.

Holly turned and smiled at her. 'You're probably right, Sinead. And it is ages since I went out.'

'Right, now that we've sorted out your feelings of guilt, let's go down to the men. They'll be starting to get impatient.'

Together they made their way downstairs to where Flynn and Ross were waiting for them.

Both men stood up as the girls entered the lounge. 'You look wonderful,' Ross said immediately, his eyes never leaving Holly as she walked towards him.

She smiled shyly. 'Thank you.'

DIVIDED BY LOVE

'And Sinead, you look stunning,' Flynn murmured.

The note in his voice caused Holly to glance round at him with a smile. 'I think she looks like Scarlett O'Hara in *Gone with the Wind*.'

This caused Sinead to burst into peals of laughter. 'Which one of you men would fancy yourself as Rhett Butler?'

'As Ross is your brother, it will have to be me.' Flynn stepped forward and held out his arm for her. 'Allow me, Miss Scarlett.'

With a playful curtsy, Sinead took hold of his arm and they led the way out of the farmhouse towards Ross's car.

Sinead did look very beautiful. She was dark and vivacious. Her long straight hair fell in a shining bell to her shoulders. Her dress was a deep cherry-red.

Holly knew that the only reason her brother had agreed to go to the ball tonight was because Ross had assured him that Sinead would be coming with them. Her brother had always liked Sinead. She on the other hand had always looked on Flynn as just Holly's little brother.

The girls sat in the back of the car, the men in the front. They set off for Lord Ashling's estate in high spirits.

The summer ball had come to be a tradition over the last few years. The young lord, Jonathan Ashling, was very popular in the community, and he enjoyed throwing a big party in a very grand style.

'I wonder what he'll do this year?' Sinead asked now. 'Jonathan usually has a few surprises lined up. Last year everything had a Caribbean theme ... do you remember those rum punches and the limbo dancing?' Sinead smiled dreamily. 'Quin gave me a lift home.'

Holly's smile faded at the mention of Quinlan. It was two weeks now since she had marched up to Quinlan's house. She hadn't seen him since and he still hadn't sent her a bill for the fence. She wondered if he was going to be at the ball tonight, and if she should broach the subject with him if he was.

The car turned through the large wrought-iron gates with the Ashling family crests engraved over the top. Then it was another twenty minutes before the dark shadowy silhouette of the house came into sight.

Usually lights blazed from the huge old house right across the lawns. Tonight, however, the lighting was more subdued. There was an unusual orange-yellow glow from the large Georgian windows.

Ross found a parking space around the back of the house and they walked round to the front door. As soon as Flynn pressed the bell the large double doors swung open.

The house was completely lit by candlelight. Silver candelabra were everywhere, giving the illusion of stepping back into time. As usual the crowd were elegantly dressed, the women in long dresses, the men in dark dinner suits. This year, however, they all wore masks. The women held ornately decorated ones; the men wore dark ones across their eyes.

Sinead laughed gaily and led the way across to where a member of Lord Ashling's staff was handing the masks out.

'What a fabulous idea,' Holly remarked as she took a mask with touches of blue in it to match her dress.

'I love these parties,' Sinead said with a gleam in her eyes as they walked through the entrance hall towards the ballroom.

This room was also lit by candles. A huge crystal chandelier of them blazed from the high ceiling. Couples were dancing to a Strauss waltz played by a small orchestra at the far end of the room.

'I wonder if Quin is here yet?' Sinead mused idly as they all helped themselves to drinks from a passing waiter.

'That is the second time this evening that you've mentioned Quinlan,' Holly said with a frown.

Sinead grimaced. 'Sorry, Hol... I thought it was all right to mention Quin now. Someone told me that the rift between the Fitzgeralds and the Montgomery had finally come to an end.'

'Well, that someone has got it wrong,' Holly said, sending Ross a disapproving look. 'There is about as much chance of the rift between our families healing as there is of my bungy-jumping off Sugar Loaf.'

Sinead laughed. 'You shouldn't have said that, Holly. I've got this picture in my head now of you leaping off that mountain in your blue silk dress.'

'Holly is not leaping anywhere but into my arms for the next dance,' Ross interjected drily. He held out a hand towards her with a smile.

'Only on the condition that you stop filling your sister's head with such rubbish,' Holly said with a smile as she put her glass down.

'It wasn't me, Holly.' He led her through the crowds of people towards the dance-floor. 'I haven't said a word to her about your entertaining Quinlan at the farm.'

'I wasn't entertaining him.' She glared up at him. 'I told you, he brought Flynn home.'

'Ah, yes,' Ross murmured with a smile as he took her into his arms. He held her close as they wove their way among the other dancers.

'If it wasn't you who put that ridiculous idea into Sinead's head, then who was it?' Holly asked suddenly.

'No idea.' Ross shrugged. 'Anyway,' he continued, bending his head close to her ear, 'let's forget Quinlan for a moment. I'm glad you've come this evening.'

'I am, too.' She smiled up at him. 'You were right, I did need to get out and have a break from the farm.'

He nodded. 'I think it's done Flynn a world of good as well.'

'Yes, he looks happier than I've seen him in a long time.' She turned her head and searched for her tall, handsome brother across the crowded room.

Instead of her eyes encountering Flynn, they landed on Quinlan Montgomery. He looked sensational in his dark evening suit. It seemed to emphasise the broad width of his shoulders, the dark gleam of his hair.

He turned as if sensing her eyes on him and looked directly at her. The dark mask across his eyes gave him the appearance of having just stepped out from another era. It made him look slightly sinister, as if he was about to go out and hold up a stagecoach or something. Holly shivered and glanced hurriedly away from him.

'Are you all right?' Ross looked down at her with concern as he felt the tremor race through her body.

'Fine.' Holly smiled up at him and forced the disturbing image of Quinlan from her mind. 'It's very warm in here actually. Shall we skip the next dance and go and get a drink?'

He agreed immediately and they rejoined Flynn and Sinead, who were deep in discussion.

'No, no, the feud between us and the Montgomerys started when Darcy Montgomery raped Lucinda Fitzgerald,' Flynn was saying heatedly.

'For goodness' sake!' Holly complained with exasperation. 'Don't you think it's about time you dropped the subject of the Montgomery family?'

Sinead shook her head. 'Not really. I find the subject fascinating.'

'You mean you find Quinlan Montgomery fascinating,' her brother put in with a laugh.

'Yes, I do.' Sinead nodded with a grin. 'He has a physique that makes my heart go into overdrive.'

'I think it was Shakespeare who said, "The devil hath power to assume a pleasing shape,"' Holly retorted cryptically.

'Are you sure he wasn't referring to a woman at the time?' Ross asked with a grin, then nudged Holly. 'Talking of your devil...' There was a note of warning in his voice.

Holly looked around and her heart sank as she saw Quinlan making his way towards them. He had an attractive blonde by his side. She wore a clinging red dress that showed a very curvy figure to its best advantage.

'Good evening, Quin.' Ross was the first to greet the other man.

'Ross.' Quin nodded and his eyes swept around all of them. 'Are you enjoying the party?' His glance lingered for a moment on Holly.

It was on the tip of her tongue to say that she had been up until now, but she refrained. She would just ignore him as she usually did.

'We certainly are.' It was Sinead who answered him, and she glanced curiously at the woman next to him.

'I don't think you've met my sister-in-law, Fiona Matthews,' Quinlan introduced the woman smoothly.

Holly looked at the woman with renewed interest, as did Sinead.

She had flawless classical features. Her honey-blonde hair was thick and luxuriant. Holly could see the resemblance now between her and Camilla Montgomery, Quinlan's deceased wife. There was the same coolness in the ice-blue eyes, the same regal poise.

'Pleased to meet you, Fiona.' Ross offered his hand in a firm handshake.

Holly noticed the woman's hand flashed fire under the gleam of candlelight with a most magnificent diamond bracelet.

'Flynn Fitzgerald?' Fiona paused over the name as Quin introduced her around one by one. 'That name is familiar.'

'My next-door neighbour,' Quin supplied drily.

'Ah... Fitzgerald. My sister used to talk of you.' The woman's frown disappeared and she smiled.

'I can imagine,' Flynn grinned.

Before Quin got around to introducing Holly, Lord Ashling appeared beside them and the conversation changed track.

Jonathan Ashling was probably the same age as Quinlan, about thirty-five. He was attractive in a rakish kind of way, tall and slimly built. His sandy hair was thinning a little at the front but it didn't detract at all from his looks. He had a charming personality and most people instantly liked him.

'Hope you're all enjoying the party.' He smiled around at them all.

'It's wonderful,' Sinead enthused immediately.

'I am glad.' Jonathan's eyes lighted on Holly. 'And I'm pleased to see you here tonight, Holly. How are things?' His voice was low and there was a concerned light in the steady grey eyes that made Holly realise he was referring to how she was coping since her parents' death.

'We're managing, thank you, Jonathan,' she said quietly.

'Holly does more than manage,' Quinlan interrupted. 'Her parents would be very proud of the way she has been able to take over at the farm.'

Holly glared at him. What on earth had prompted him to say that? How dared he make such a personal statement? And apart from the fact that it was personal, he made it sound as if Flynn had nothing to do with the farm at all, so it was a remark that was bound to make Flynn feel bad. Her brother needed his confidence building up at the moment, not tearing down. '*Flynn* and I do our best.' She deliberately emphasised her brother's name.

'Well, don't hesitate to contact me if you need any help or advice.' Jonathan smiled, then turned towards Quinlan.

The conversation turned towards farming and Sinead made a face at Holly. 'Nothing so boring as farming,' she said in a low voice.

'Actually I quite enjoy it,' Holly said truthfully.

'Yes, but you must miss life in Dublin,' her friend insisted. 'I'd go mad if I had to be cooped up in the country all the time again. I love the theatres and the restaurants and the shops.'

'So does Holly,' Flynn interjected from beside her, and there was no mistaking the note of guilt in his voice. 'I wish I could sell the damn place and liberate us both.'

'Flynn!' Holly sent him a warning glance. She didn't want everyone overhearing such a comment. 'You know I'm happy to be at home.'

'You are not happy, Holly. You just have a misplaced sense of loyalty to the land... to me.' He fell silent after that and it was obvious that his cheerful mood had deserted him and once more he was brooding about being tied to the farm.

Anxiety clouded her eyes and she glanced away from him straight into Quin's sparkling blue gaze. This was all his fault. She just hoped that he had been too busy listening to Jonathan to hear what Flynn had said. It would be just the last straw for Quinlan Montgomery to know all their business.

'Would you like to dance, Holly?' Quin asked, throwing her completely.

Before she had a chance to say anything, Sinead had placed a hand at her back and was slightly pushing her forward towards him.

'Sinead!' She turned her eyes towards her friend, a gleam of annoyance on her face. Unfortunately Quinlan seemed to take the fact that she had moved towards him as acceptance. He took hold of her hand and before she realised what he was doing he was leading her out towards the floor.

'Let go of my hand, Quinlan,' she demanded in a low tone, trying not to create a scene.

He ignored the words and merely grinned at her. 'This should cause a few tongues to wag—a Montgomery and a Fitzgerald having a dance.' He rolled his eyes in a mocking manner. 'Outrageously daring. I bet there hasn't been such an occurrence since Darcy Montgomery danced with Lucinda all those generations ago.'

'Lucinda Fitzgerald never danced with that rat,' Holly told him in a very stern tone.

'No?' He raised an eyebrow. 'I think you're wrong there, and dancing isn't all they did,' he finished in a low mocking tone.

Holly's face flushed with hot, furious colour at such a comment.

He released her hand as they reached the dance-floor and turned to face her. 'So are you going to have this dance with me or are you too scared?'

'Scared?' Her voice lifted at such an outrageous question. 'I'm not afraid of you,' she told him in a haughty tone.

'Good.' He smiled. 'Then let's not disappoint everyone.'

So saying, he gathered her into his arms and together they moved in among the other couples.

Holly was very aware of everyone watching them. For a moment it seemed that a hush descended on the crowded room, but maybe that was her imagination, or maybe her heart was beating so loudly in her ears that it blocked out all the other noises in the room.

Quinlan's arms were firm on her waist and on her shoulder. They seemed to Holly to be burning into her like two bands of steel.

'There's no need to hold me quite so close,' she told him, raising her head to look at him.

'I think there's every need,' he grinned. 'You look beautiful tonight, Holly.'

Much to her annoyance, her skin flushed an even brighter red at the compliment. Why it should have thrown her so completely she had no idea; after all, she didn't care one jot about Quin Montgomery's opinions.

The blue eyes seemed to laugh down at her as he noted the high colour in her cheeks. 'Why, Holly, I do believe I've made you blush.'

'Don't be ridiculous,' she snapped. 'I'm a little hot, that's all.'

'Really? Perhaps you would like to step outside and we can take some fresh air together?' There was a suggestive undertone in the velvet-deep voice that made Holly's skin grow even hotter.

'I don't want to step anywhere with you,' she retorted furiously. 'In fact, I would rather not breathe the same air as you.'

He laughed at the vehemence of her reply. It was a rich, attractive sound and it turned a few women's heads instantly towards him. His head bent towards hers and she stiffened as his mouth came close to her ear. 'Holly Fitzgerald, you're priceless,' he whispered in a humorous undertone. 'It's a long time since I've found a woman who entertains and amuses me so totally.'

Her body stiffened at that galling remark. 'It wasn't my intention to entertain you, Montgomery,' she snapped heatedly. 'My intention was to insult you.'

'I know, but you do it so beautifully.' The blue eyes sparkled with mirth. 'I had thought that I wanted a truce to be called between us, but now I'm not so sure. It's much more fun to wind you up and watch you explode, especially if I'm holding you in my arms at the time.'

'I beg your pardon?' Holly's voice shook with indignation. How dared this man speak to her in such a manner? She was practically speechless, she was so intensely angry. She tried to pull away from him but his arms just tightened more around her. 'Let me go,' she demanded through clenched teeth.

He shook his head. 'We haven't finished our dance yet.'

'Oh, yes, we have,' Holly grated, a determined light suddenly entering her dark eyes. She didn't stop to think about her actions; temper drove her to swing her foot and aim a discreet but sharp kick on his shin.

For a moment she thought he was going to physically attack her. A gleam of anger frosted his blue eyes for the first time. 'That was not a good idea.' His voice was low and yet there was an ominous tone to it. Holly could feel her anger dissolving into apprehension.

'Perhaps you had better apologise,' he continued.

They stood stock-still in the middle of the dance-floor, the other couples whirling around them and sending curious glances in their direction.

'And if I don't?' She angled her chin upwards and met his eyes, her pride hanging on even in the midst of her fear.

The arrogant strong mouth twisted into an amused smile. 'You'll have to wait and see, won't you?'

The taunting words made her blood boil. 'I'll not apologise to a Montgomery,' she told him, blithely throwing caution to the winds. She was damned if she was going to say she was sorry when he was in the wrong. He should have let her go when she had asked him.

'Please yourself.' That sparkle of humour was back in his eyes. Then the firm hands at her back and her waist turned her and she thought he was going to continue forcing her to dance with him. But he intended worse than that, much worse.

It was only when his dark head started to lower straight towards her that his intention dawned on her, and by then it was too late to turn her head away.

One hand moved to the back of her head and held her firmly while his lips covered hers in a kiss so forceful, so passionate that her breath seemed to freeze in her throat.

Even while it was happening Holly could hardly believe it. Quinlan Montgomery was kissing her in the middle of the dance-floor... in full view of the whole community. It was demeaning... hateful. The touch of his lips crushing the softness of hers was like a slow kind of torture. She would make him pay for this, she vowed furiously... Quinlan Montgomery would rue the day he had decided to make a laughing-stock out of her.

He released her abruptly and she stood staring up into those midnight-blue eyes with furious fires of hatred burning inside her.

His hand reached up and touched the side of her cheek in a curiously gentle gesture. She was sure he could feel the full force of her outrage radiating through the softness of her skin.

His lips curved in a smile. 'Yes,' he murmured in a low husky tone that was barely audible. 'I especially like it when you explode in my arms.' Then he turned and left her standing there.

Holly glanced at the couples still dancing around the floor, aware of the curious glances they were throwing her, the whispers. It was intolerable, she thought furiously... intolerable. Then, with her head held high, she marched from the floor with as much dignity as her shaking limbs could muster.

The group of people whose company she had left were all watching her as she walked back to them. She was very aware of the expression on each of their faces. Ross looked sad somehow, and she couldn't quite work out why he should look at her like that. Her brother and Sinead were staring at her with open mouths. Her glance would have swept over Quinlan's sister-in-law without any interest at all except for the look in the woman's eyes.

'Vicious' was the word that sprung to Holly's mind as she met Fiona Matthews' gaze head-on. There was no doubt about it—the other woman was livid with anger at what she had just witnessed. Why? Holly mused with a feeling of foreboding? Why should Fiona be so powerfully upset by Quinlan kissing her; was it out of deference to Camilla's memory? Quinlan's wife had been dead for a number of years now, so surely Fiona couldn't still feel so acutely agonised by the knowledge that her brother-in-law was free to do as he wished where women were concerned?

As Holly reached them Fiona turned on her heel and walked away. Holly let her breath out in a sigh of relief; she wasn't up to any more heated confrontations. She had had quite enough for one night.

'It's OK, you can close your mouths now.' Holly managed to toss the comment in a humorous way at her brother and Sinead, who were still staring at her incredulously.

'I'm as jealous as hell.' Sinead was the first to speak. Her lips stretched into a grin and she shook her head. 'And you were the one who told us that you had no intention of patching things up with Quinlan,' she said curiously. 'What happened?'

'Nothing happened.' Holly reached for the glass of orange she had left on the table next to them.

'Come on, Sis!' Flynn said in a puzzled tone. 'Something happened out there. We all saw you kissing Montgomery.'

Holly swung furious eyes on her brother. 'No... you saw Montgomery kissing me... there is a difference.'

'If you say so.' Flynn shrugged but sounded totally unconvinced.

'Well, at least you shut the snooty Ms Matthews up.' Sinead giggled. 'You should have seen her face.'

'Actually, I did notice that she looked less than amused,' Holly remarked.

'If you ask me, she has designs on Quin,' Sinead said morosely now. 'She's just been telling us that she has come down from Dublin for the summer to help out with Jamie. Apparently Quinlan's childminder has left to get married and Aunty Fiona is stepping into the breach. Reading between the lines, I'd say that dear Aunty Fiona is only interested in helping herself... to Quinlan.'

'With all due respect, sometimes you're not that good at reading between lines,' Holly said wryly. 'For instance, Quin and me. There is nothing going on and I still regard him as my mortal enemy.'

Sinead laughed. 'OK, point taken. But if that's how you treat your mortal enemies...' She let the words trail off tantalisingly.

'Stop teasing, Sinead,' Ross interrupted suddenly, and there was a strangely sharp note to his voice. 'If Holly says there's nothing going on, then that's what she means.'

'All right, all right. I won't say another word.' Sinead rolled her eyes. 'Come on, Flynn, let's have a dance before my big brother snaps my head off.'

Flynn grinned and took her arm, only too pleased to comply with that request.

Holly sipped her drink and glanced around the room. Where had Quin gone? she found herself wondering. Her heartbeats seemed to have returned to normal now, but somehow she imagined that she could still feel the pressure of his mouth on hers. It would take a while to recover from that man's outrageous behaviour, she thought angrily.

She glanced back and found Ross watching her, a strange expression on his face.

'So...?' He hesitated. 'What was it all about?'

'What?' She looked up at him with innocent eyes.

'Come on, Holly. I'm talking about you and Quin. What really passed between you out there?'

'Nothing.' Holly shook her head. 'I really don't want to talk about it, Ross. Suffice it to say that Quinlan Montgomery is a hateful man.'

'All right.' He shrugged. 'Would you like to go through to the other room and get something to eat from the buffet?'

She nodded, very relieved that the subject had been dropped.

The rest of the evening passed in a hazy whirl of dancing and light-hearted conversation. Holly didn't see Quin again until it was coming up to midnight.

Flynn had disappeared off somewhere, much to Holly's annoyance. She was ready to leave, as was Ross and Sinead. All of them had early starts in the morning.

'Sorry, Ross,' Holly said as she saw him glancing at his watch again. 'I'll go and see if he's in the other room.'

The party was still in full swing. The dance-floor was completely packed now and the overflow of people from the ballroom spilled out to the dining-room and the hallway. Holly went from room to room several times but there was no sign of Flynn.

She was standing at the base of the stairway wondering if he was upstairs, when the door through to Lord Ashling's study opened and she saw Flynn standing in there. At first she thought he was talking to Jonathan. There was a serious expression on his young face. 'I'll give it some thought,' she heard him say clearly as the door opened even wider.

She moved across. 'Flynn, I've been——' She cut off abruptly as she saw that he wasn't speaking to Jonathan at all. It was Quinlan who stood at the other side of the room.

'I've been looking for you.' She forced herself to look away from Quin's sparkling gaze and straight at Flynn. 'We're ready to leave.'

'Right, I'm coming.' He glanced back at Quinlan. 'I'll be in touch.'

Holly frowned over at Quin and he grinned at her.

'See you around.'

'Not if I see you first.' She turned to go after Flynn, conscious of the laughter that followed her.

Flynn very carefully avoided her eyes as she caught up with him.

'What was all that about?' she asked curiously.

He shrugged. 'A bit of business.'

'Business!' She looked up at him, totally perplexed. 'What business could you possibly have with a Montgomery?'

He glanced down at her then. 'Nothing that need concern you, sister dear,' he muttered in a condescending tone.

Holly frowned, angry at that patronising statement, but she said nothing more. It was obvious that Flynn wasn't going to tell her anything more than that. He was very wrong when he said it didn't concern her, though, she thought drily. It concerned her a lot. She had a very uneasy feeling that something was terribly wrong.

CHAPTER FOUR

GREYSTONES harbour nestled in the curve of the bay, flanked by Bray Head and a wide sweeping beach. A hazy mist hung over the cornflower-blue of the sea, and the boats rested calmly in the harbour, hardly a ripple disturbing their reflections in the satin-smooth water.

For a moment Holly's eyes rested on the peaceful scene. As a child she had played on that beach for hours on end, hide-and-seek in the fishermen's boats that were pulled high away from the water, swimming parties, barbecues. She smiled as she remembered those carefree days. She was lucky to have had such an idyllic childhood, such good parents. For a moment her eyes clouded over as she thought about her parents. She missed them so much.

Resolutely she turned her Land Rover back towards the farm. There was no time to get maudlin. She had picked up the week's shopping in record time and now there were a million jobs awaiting her attention back at the farm.

It was going to be another scorching-hot day, she thought as her car sped along the country lanes. Already a shimmering haze was dancing over the road in front. It had been a wonderful summer, long, hot months with hardly any rain, and it looked as if August was going to continue in the same vein, most unusually, for the Irish summer was usually a very mixed affair of soft damp days and sunny interludes. She loved the hot weather, but it did make physical work much more tiring.

The car rounded a sharp bend in the road and then much to her dismay started to lose power.

'Damn!' Her voice was loud in the still summer air as the engine died completely. She managed to free-wheel in to the side of the road and then she released the bonnet and got out to have a look.

The lane was quiet except for the occasional call of a blackbird sitting on a hedge of sweet-smelling honeysuckle. Holly flicked a glance over at him. 'What am I going to do now?' she asked in a tone half humorous, half vexed. She didn't know anything about engines, she was miles away from home, and just to make matters worse all the groceries in the Land Rover would probably go off sitting in this heat.

The throaty purr of a car answered her question and she looked up, hoping fervently that it would be someone she knew and preferably someone who knew something about cars.

A shining red Ferrari pulled alongside and Holly's heart sank as she saw it was Fiona Matthews who sat behind the driving-wheel.

'Having problems?' she asked in crystal-cool tones.

'You could say that,' Holly answered wryly. 'My car seems to have died a death.'

'I see.' The woman frowned. 'Didn't we meet last night at Lord Ashling's party?'

Holly nodded. 'Holly Fitzgerald,' she refreshed the woman's memory, although she was sure that Fiona had not forgotten her.

'Ah, yes.' Fiona smiled. 'Our next-door neighbour. I remember Quin telling me all about you last night.'

It all sounded very cosy, Holly thought drily. As if she was living at Montgomery House for good, not just staying on holiday.

Holly's eyes moved to the passenger seat of the Ferrari. She had Jamie Montgomery with her. He met her glance with a small smile. There was something about that smile that touched Holly's heart. She didn't know if she was imagining things, but she thought that she could see deep unhappiness in that little boy's face.

'Hello, Jamie,' she said in a cheerful tone.

'Hello...' The child frowned for a moment before recognition set in. 'You were going to hide with me from Daddy,' he murmured, the beginnings of a grin playing around his mouth now.

Despite her problems Holly had to laugh. 'That's right.'

'You didn't come to my birthday party,' he said now, taking Holly very much by surprise. 'Didn't Daddy ask you?'

'Well, yes, he did, Jamie, but I'm afraid I had something else on.' As she spoke the white lie she felt incredibly guilty somehow, as if she had let the child down. It was a crazy feeling; she hardly knew Jamie Montgomery.

'Do stop grousing, Jamie,' Fiona cut across the conversation, an impatient note in her voice. She pushed her sunglasses up into her silky blonde hair and glanced at Holly sharply. 'I'm sorry, but I really don't know anything about car engines, so I can't be of any help.'

'That's all right.' Holly shrugged good-naturedly. 'I don't know anything about engines myself.'

'I'll tell Daddy we've seen you,' Jamie said to her with a smile.

Holly wouldn't have been surprised if Fiona had just driven off at that point, but instead she hesitated, then said crisply, 'If it's any help I could run you home.'

The offer startled Holly. 'Well, that would be nice,' she murmured. 'I do have a lot of shopping that should go straight into the fridge.'

'I'll open the boot.' Fiona sounded less than pleased, as if the whole thing was really too much trouble... but then maybe that was just her imagination, Holly thought; after all, it was very good of Fiona to offer her a lift.

She pulled the Ferrari in front and propped open the boot. Then she got out and stood watching while Holly unloaded the heavy bags one by one into the back. She made no attempt to help, Holly noticed wryly.

Jamie also climbed out and he came running around to her. He looked very cute in a pale blue pair of chinos and a white short-sleeved shirt. 'Shall I take something for you, Holly?' he asked her helpfully.

Holly smiled down at him. 'That's very good of you, Jamie, but I think these bags are a bit heavy for you.' Holly picked another plastic carrier up and he tried to take hold of one corner with her.

'Jamie, for heaven's sake get out of the way,' Fiona snapped at him immediately.

'He's all right,' Holly quickly assured her.

'I help my dad sometimes when he's doing the shopping,' Jamie told her happily.

Somehow Holly found it hard to picture Quin Montgomery doing any shopping.

'He's going to take me for a picnic on Saturday,' Jamie continued to chatter. 'Would you like to come, Holly?'

Before Holly had a chance to answer that disconcerting question, Fiona answered for her.

'Holly will have better things to do with her time, and anyway I think we'll have to cancel your picnic. Your father is coming into Dublin with me on Saturday.' The woman's voice was abrasively sharp. 'Now get back into the car, Jamie, and try to keep quiet for a while.'

The boy turned to do as he was told, a crestfallen look on the little face.

Holly thought that the woman was unnecessarily sharp with him, but she said nothing, just finished loading her bags and then locked up the Land Rover.

The journey back to the farm was made in near silence. Fiona speeded along the country lanes with a look of determination on her beautiful face.

'You wouldn't believe how troublesome that boy is,' she muttered to Holly at one point. 'I've told Quinlan that he should see about placing him in a boarding-school. It would teach him some discipline and it would be so much easier for Quin.'

Holly felt a surge of anger at that comment. It didn't seem right to make such a statement when the five-year-old in question was sitting beside them. She glanced around at him. The expression on his young face was so bleak that it made her want to gather him into her arms and tell Fiona to shut up.

They turned in through the gateposts to the farm and Holly turned her attention away from the boy. It was none of her business, she told herself forcibly.

The farmhouse came into sight and to her annoyance she noticed Quin's Range Rover parked outside the front door. What did he want? she wondered. Perhaps he had called to give them the bill for the fence?

'Daddy's car, Daddy's car!' Jamie suddenly sprang to excited life as the car stopped.

Holly opened the door and got out and he was out beside her in a minute. 'Can I go and see if he's in your house, Holly?'

She nodded at him. A strange feeling of apprehension was creeping through her. If Quin was just dropping off a bill he didn't need to go into the house. He could have given it to Flynn on the doorstep.

The boy went running off and Holly turned to get her shopping from the car.

'Does Quin drop over here often?' Fiona asked with a frown as she came around to stand beside her.

'No.' Holly struggled to pick two bags up at once and as she turned Quinlan appeared in the doorway.

'Well, this is a nice surprise.' His eyes swept from Fiona to Holly and he grinned.

For some reason Holly was suddenly acutely aware of the difference between Fiona and herself. Fiona was dressed in a beautiful cream linen suit with a long line jacket and short skirt that showed her golden-brown legs to great advantage. Holly on the other hand just wore a faded pair of 501 jeans and a white cotton T-shirt.

'Here, let me take those for you.' Quin crossed towards her and reached out for the shopping bags.

For a moment Holly was tempted to refuse his help, but his hands were already on the bags and she didn't really relish a tug of war in front of the cool, sophisticated Fiona, so she relinquished them reluctantly. 'What are you doing here?' she asked in what she hoped was a disdainful voice.

'I came to see your brother.' He turned and headed into the house with the bags of shopping.

'What for?' She followed close on his heels.

'I suggest you ask Flynn.' He flicked an amused glance over his shoulder at her. 'By the way, I've been admiring that portrait of you in the lounge.'

She glowered at him. 'That's not me, it's...' She trailed off, suddenly realising that he knew very well it was Lucinda Fitzgerald, that he was teasing her. 'You know very well who it is,' she finished irately.

'Actually I did think it was you at first,' Quin admitted with a smile as he put her bags on the kitchen table. 'It was Flynn who told me that it was Lucinda. The resemblance is remarkable.'

'Who is Lucinda?' Fiona asked from behind them.

'One of Holly's relatives from generations past,' Quin answered her. 'Why don't you go into the lounge and have a look?'

'Is she the one who fell in love with a Montgomery?' Fiona asked curiously.

'One and the same.' Quin noticed the furious look on Holly's face and grinned. 'I think Holly is about to disagree with me again.'

'Because you're twisting the facts,' Holly told him heatedly.

'Well, we won't go into that now.' Quin disappeared from the room to go and get the rest of the shopping.

'That man drives me mad,' Holly muttered under her breath. She looked over at Fiona and found she was watching her with a look of deep contemplation.

'Are you in love with Quinlan?' Fiona asked her coolly.

The question shook Holly, it was so totally unexpected and so ludicrous. 'Certainly not!' she said emphatically. 'What on earth made you ask that?'

The woman shrugged. 'I don't know, something about the way you look at him, the way sparks seem to fly when you're around him.'

'Sparks fly because I don't really like the man,' Holly said with a determined shake of her auburn hair. 'No other reason.'

Fiona nodded. 'It's just as well,' she said drily. 'You would only get hurt.' With that the woman turned and walked out of the room.

What was that supposed to mean? Holly wondered. Was it some kind of warning? She shrugged the whole thing off. The most pressing thing at the moment was to find out why Quin had been in the house.

She found Flynn in the lounge talking to Jamie. Fiona had perched herself on the settee beside him. Holly noticed that the coffee-pot and two cups sat on the table. Obviously Quin had been having a coffee with Flynn when their arrival had interrupted them. Had their conversation had anything to do with what they had been discussing last night at the party? Holly wondered uneasily.

Flynn looked up as she came in and Holly thought that he looked a little guilty as he met her eye. 'You got back from town early,' he said.

'Only thanks to Fiona. My car broke down on the way home.'

Flynn stood up immediately. 'Where is it? I'll go and see if I can sort it out.'

'It's a couple of miles back down the road, but don't rush off,' Holly said calmly. 'First, why don't you tell me what Quinlan wanted?'

Silence met the question for a moment, then he shrugged. 'Nothing, Sis. We were just having a chat about some farming business.'

Holly frowned. 'You mean the bill for the fence?'

'That's right.' He seemed to seize upon the idea almost too quickly, as if it was just the excuse that he had been desperately searching for.

Holly glanced around as Quinlan came to stand in the doorway. 'So how much do we owe you for the fence?' she asked him drily.

He shrugged and there was a look of amusement on the handsome features. 'Flynn and I will come to an agreement, don't worry about it.'

Was it her imagination, or was there a strange undercurrent to those words? Holly was far from pleased with that answer but there was little she could say.

'Dad, are we still going on our picnic on Saturday?' Jamie suddenly piped into the conversation.

Quin looked over at his son and smiled. 'Yes, Jamie.'

Fiona shook back her hair and looked up at him appealingly. 'But, Quin, I'm going into Dublin for the day on Saturday. There are one or two things I need to pick up from my house. I thought you might like to come with me.'

'Sorry, Fiona.' Quin shook his head. 'I had already promised Jamie, and I don't break promises lightly.'

'I see.' Fiona's face clouded over. 'Well, I guess I'll just have to go on my own.' She was obviously less than pleased but Quin didn't seem to have any intention of weakening.

For a moment Holly felt like cheering. At least Quin had some principles. Her eyes moved over his lean handsome face and for the first time she wondered if he wasn't quite so black as she had always painted him. He seemed to be a good father to Jamie, and the boy obviously adored him.

'Well, I'll be getting back to the house.' Fiona got to her feet and looked down at the child. 'Are you coming, Jamie?' she asked crisply.

Jamie shook his head.

'Go on, Jamie,' Quin said briskly. 'I can't take you home just yet—I've one or two other calls to make first.'

The boy got up obediently. 'All right, then.' He sounded resigned as he went across and gave his father a kiss, then to Holly's surprise he came across and gave her a kiss too. 'Goodbye, Holly.'

'Bye, sweetheart.'

Fiona caught hold of his hand as they went out and Holly didn't care for the look on her face. She was furious.

'I don't think Fiona is too pleased with you,' she remarked as the woman closed the front door.

'She'll get over it,' Quinlan said nonchalantly.

'How long is she staying with you?' Flynn asked him, and Holly sent him a fulminating glance. What on earth had possessed him to ask such a personal question?

Quinlan shrugged. 'I don't know; she hasn't decided. I hope she'll stay for quite a while.'

Holly moved towards the door; she had heard enough. 'If you'll excuse me, I have a lot of work to see to,' she said coolly.

She made her way to the kitchen and was putting all the groceries away when Quinlan appeared in the doorway.

'Haven't you gone yet?' she asked as she turned and found him watching her.

Instead of answering, he just smiled. This irritated Holly further. 'I really don't want you in my house, Quin,' she told him heatedly.

'But it's not really your house, is it, Holly?' he answered her smoothly.

'Of course it's my house.' Her eyes flashed fire at him. 'What kind of a stupid statement is that?' she demanded angrily. 'This is my home, the place I grew up in.'

He shrugged. 'And then you moved out and went to live in Dublin,' he reminded her calmly.

'Well, that was because I was working in Dublin,' Holly said with a frown. 'Now I'm working back at home.'

'But only temporarily to help Flynn out,' Quin continued patiently. 'The farm is his. I suppose once he's got his life back in order you'll want to go back to Dublin.'

'For your information, I'm very happy being back home,' Holly told him in no uncertain terms. 'Not that it's any of your business.'

He shrugged. 'Maybe not, but I do know a lot about farming and I know this place is too much for a woman to manage on her own.'

'I'm not on my own.' Holly slanted her chin firmly up. 'I have Flynn... remember?'

He chose not to answer that. 'I still think you're working too hard,' he said instead.

Holly glared at him. 'I'm coping perfectly.' She turned and continued on with her work, hoping he would leave.

He continued to stand and watch her. 'How about having dinner with me tonight?' he asked suddenly.

She whirled around to look at him. 'Are you being funny?' she asked him scornfully. 'I'd rather have dinner with the devil himself than dine with you.'

One eyebrow lifted at that. 'Do you know what I think, Holly Fitzgerald?' he asked softly in a teasing voice.

'I don't want to know what you think,' she said with a shake of her head.

He continued on regardless. 'I think that you're afraid of me. I think you've always been afraid of me, that the old feud between our families is just an excuse for you to tell yourself you don't like me.'

'I don't need an excuse,' Holly told him heatedly. 'And I'm certainly not afraid of you, Quinlan Montgomery.'

'Prove it. Have dinner with me tomorrow night.' He threw down the invitation like a golden challenge for her to pick up.

Holly shook her head and refused to be drawn. 'I don't have to prove anything.'

'Not even to yourself?' he asked mockingly.

'Especially to myself.' She glared at him defiantly. 'Now please get off Fitzgerald land.'

'Your brother invited me on to his land,' Quin told her pointedly. 'I don't think that's any way to talk to his guest.'

Holly stared at him bewildered. Flynn had invited him here today... why? The question burned inside her.

'You see, Holly, your brother doesn't hold with this feudal thing. He feels no real antagonism for the Montgomery name. It is only you who clings to an episode from the past with such stubborn rancour. Have you ever stopped to ask yourself why?' With that he turned and left her alone in the kitchen.

Holly's heart was thundering against her breast as if she had been running a race. She wasn't afraid of Quinlan Montgomery, she told herself fiercely. The very idea made her blood boil. She had a very good reason to dislike him. Her father had told her the story of Darcy Montgomery and Lucinda Fitzgerald when she'd been just a child. It had stayed with her just as it must have stayed with her father and his father before him. It was a lesson well learnt, a lesson on not to trust a Montgomery. Resolutely she went to find Flynn; she wanted to know exactly what was going on.

He was outside next to the Range Rover, talking with Quin. Holly lingered in the doorway; she didn't want to join in with whatever they were talking about. What *were* they talking about? The question haunted her.

They were much the same height, Holly noted idly as she waited. Quin was more powerfully built than her brother, though. He had wider shoulders, a tougher angle to his jawline. He was dressed in smarter clothes as well, but then Quin Montgomery wasn't a farmer in the true sense of the word. He had a manager and a full team of labourers on his farm. Added to that, he had enjoyed enormous success training and breeding racehorses. Quinlan probably spent his days counting his money, she thought sardonically. He was a businessman through and through.

She waited until Quin got into his vehicle and drove away before crossing the yard towards her brother.

'What did he want?' she asked him again, very bluntly this time.

Flynn glanced down at her. 'I told you,' he said and then turned towards the stables.

'No, you didn't, you told me some excuse about him coming to drop in a bill.' Holly followed him determinedly. 'Quin told me that you invited him over here. Is that true?'

Flynn sighed. 'Yes, Holly, I invited him.'

'Why?'

The question remained unanswered as they went into the stables. It was cooler in there than it was outside and it was dark after the bright glare of the sunshine. Flynn went to get his saddle from the tack-room at the back. Holly stood and waited next to the horses. She wasn't going to let this go. She wanted to know the truth.

The pleasantly familiar smell of clean horse-flesh and hay mingled in the air. Betsy swished at a fly with her tail and looked at Holly with trusting eyes. She reached out a hand instinctively and stroked her velvet-soft neck.

'Why, Flynn?' she asked him again as he came back to saddle his horse. This time her voice was softer; she had calmed down a little. So what if Quin thought she was afraid of him? It wasn't true, she told herself again and again.

'Because he's our neighbour.' Flynn didn't look over at her; he just continued to buckle up the saddle as if he was only half listening.

Holly frowned. 'He's a Montgomery, Flynn,' she reminded him crisply. 'You know what Dad used to say about them.'

'Never trust a Montgomery.' Flynn sounded bored. 'Look, Holly.' He turned suddenly to face her. 'I know what Dad used to say. But I don't think he ever meant it that seriously. To be honest I think he used to say it because of how much you look like Lucinda. Perhaps he was worried that you might run off with Quinlan.' Flynn grinned at her suddenly. 'He is a very attractive man, and you are a good-looking girl.'

Holly stared at her brother as if he had suddenly gone mad.

'I believe he asked you out for dinner,' Flynn continued, unabashed.

'He told you that?' She was completely stunned. Come to think of it, why had Quin invited her out for dinner?

'You should have said yes.' He continued saddling the horse, his voice matter-of-fact.

'Why on earth should I accept an invitation from that man?' She was incensed with fury at such a ridiculous notion.

'Because he's a decent enough fellow, and anyway you don't go out enough. You've been home for six months and I don't think you've had one date in all that time.' Flynn swung himself up on to his horse.

'Well, I've been too busy.' Holly frowned up at him. 'What's the matter with you, Flynn? You don't usually concern yourself with my private life.'

Flynn shrugged. 'It was just an observation.'

'Well, I'd rather you kept your observations to yourself,' Holly said crossly. 'Anyway, I went out to the summer ball last night.'

'But that wasn't a real date,' Flynn maintained stubbornly.

'And dinner with Quinlan Montgomery would be?' Holly grated scornfully.

Flynn laughed. 'I'd say it would be real enough.' He edged his horse towards the door of the stables. 'I'm going to see if I can fix your car,' he said over his shoulder. 'See you later.'

'Hold on a minute, Flynn—I still want to know——' But her brother had gone before she could finish the sentence. She glared after him. He had successfully managed to distract her and now she was no nearer to knowing why Quinlan had been visiting.

A movement from one of the horses' stalls made her jump. 'Who's there?' she called sharply, and moved down towards the sound.

'It's only me, Holly.' One of the farm labourers stepped out from the last stall.

Holly frowned. 'How long have you been there, Nigel?'

The man shrugged. 'Not long.' He inhaled on the cigarette he was smoking and watched her with narrowed eyes through the smoke.

Holly didn't care for the insolent expression on his face; it made a shiver run down her spine. Had he been listening to her conversation? she wondered, then shrugged. It didn't really matter if he had. 'I've asked you before not to smoke in here, Nigel,' she said as the man took another drag from the cigarette.

He threw the offending item down on the floor and ground it out with his heel. Holly didn't like the way he looked at her as he did it.

'Sorry, boss,' he said sardonically then turned and walked away.

What was the matter with everyone? Holly wondered gloomily. When her father had been alive the men would never have dared to smoke in here. With a shake of her head she went to get stuck into her work for the day.

It was evening before she thought about Quinlan's visit again. She had just had a shower and put on a light cotton shirt for bed; she was exhausted and the last thing she wanted was to start worrying about Quinlan Montgomery. Yet as soon as she climbed between the sheets and closed her eyes he was there, laughing at her with those cutting blue eyes in the darkness of the summer night.

Then, more disturbing still, she found herself thinking about the way he had kissed her at the summer ball, the firm, sensual pressure of his lips against hers. She tossed and turned to escape the memory but it was insistently vivid in her mind.

Was this how the young Lucinda Fitzgerald had felt about Darcy Montgomery? The thought sprang into her mind from nowhere. Poor Lucinda, bright, vivacious, beautiful. Darcy had ruined her life, had ruthlessly taken her innocence and left her with child. Then he had scorned her, laughed at her. Lucinda had died in the third month of her pregnancy. Her father had said she had died of shame and a broken heart, a look of torment on her beautiful young face.

Holly sat bolt upright in bed, her breathing coming in short painful gasps. She must have fallen into a restless sleep because in her mind she had seen Darcy Montgomery. He had had the same blue eyes as Quinlan and he had laughed mockingly at her. 'There will be no escape for you, Holly,' he had said. 'No escape.'

Holly lay back against the softness of her pillows. It had been a silly dream, nothing more. She tried desperately to relax. Then she sat sharply up again. There was an unfamiliar noise outside, a crackling sound that made her blood run cold.

She threw the covers back and raced to the windows. The sight that met her eyes made her cry out in horror. The stables were on fire! The bright orange flames licked greedily from part of the roof into the blackness of the sky.

Holly rang for the fire brigade at the same time as tossing on a pair of tracksuit bottoms. Then, yelling for Flynn to wake up, she ran downstairs and out into the night.

A car was pulling down the drive and it pulled up just beside Holly as she stopped to watch the stables with a feeling of fear and helplessness.

Somehow she wasn't surprised to see Quinlan climbing out of his car to stand at her side.

'I saw the blaze from miles back down the road,' he said briskly. 'I've already called the fire brigade on my car phone.'

She swallowed, trying desperately to fight the panic rising inside her. 'The horses, Quin...' She turned and looked up at him with wide petrified eyes. 'Becky is fastened in; she's going to die in there.'

She glanced desperately back at the building and then without stopping to think she raced towards it. She had to get the horses out. She couldn't leave them.

'For God's sake come back.' Quinlan's rasping voice followed her but she paid it no heed.

Billowing black smoke met her at the doorway. The smell was awful; it clawed at the back of Holly's throat. She put her arm across her face to try and shield herself and then entered the raging abyss.

Despite the flames Holly could see nothing. Her vision was clouded by the smoke. But she could hear the horses; they were making high-pitched noises of distress and their hooves were pounding furiously against the doors that restricted them. Holly felt her way towards the first door and somehow she found the bolt. The horse shot out towards safety. The next stall up was Flynn's horse, then Becky. Holly was terrified but she made herself continue feeling her way along.

Flynn's black stallion was rearing against the door and pounding it with its hooves. Holly found the bolt of the door but she couldn't draw it back with one hand. She took her arm away from her nose and mouth and started immediately to cough. The bolt jerked free, and the door swung against her as the horse bolted nervously past. The force of it knocked Holly sideways and she fell to the floor, knocking her head forcefully against something as she fell.

For a moment she just lay there, dazed. She could hear Becky's high-pitched whinny over the roar of flames. The black smoke seemed to be even thicker now; it enveloped her in pitch darkness. She tried to get up, but her limbs didn't seem to want to obey her.

She looked up and wondered if she was going to die, then she saw him. It was Darcy Montgomery, she was sure of it, and he was holding out his hands towards her. Her heart pounded with fear and then she felt herself slipping into black unconsciousness.

CHAPTER FIVE

SOMEONE was saying her name over and over again. Strong arms were holding her. She was safe. Relief washed over her and she opened her eyes to find herself staring up at Quinlan. His face was very close: she could see dark flecks of grey in the blue of his eyes, a dark shadow of stubble on his tanned skin.

He brushed a strand of her auburn hair away from her face with strangely gentle fingers. 'That was a bloody foolish thing to do.' His voice was harsh, yet there was an undertone of something else in it...something that Holly couldn't quite fathom. Was it relief? Was Quinlan Montgomery concerned about her?

She swallowed hard. Her throat felt terrible, as if someone had rubbed sandpaper over it. 'The horses? Becky?' Suddenly the relief had gone, replaced with fear again as the full horror of what had happened returned.

Quinlan held her firmly as she struggled to sit up. 'They're all OK. Probably better than you.'

Holly did not feel at her best. Her eyes and her head were aching and her voice sounded very strange, husky and raw. She glanced around her anxiously.

She was lying in the yard at a safe distance from the blazing stables, Quinlan's arms supporting her. The fire brigade had arrived and seemed to be having some success in getting the fire under control. 'Where's Flynn?' she asked anxiously.

'Beats me.' Quinlan shrugged. 'Come on, let's get you inside.'

She wouldn't have been able to get to her feet except for Quinlan's help. Even when she was standing she felt dizzy. She leaned her head against his chest for a moment and then he swung her up into his arms.

She wanted to protest but suddenly it just seemed too much effort. It was easier to relax against him.

He carried her effortlessly into the house and upstairs. 'Which is your bedroom?' He hesitated on the wide landing.

'Last one on the right.' Her voice was no more than a croak.

He moved into her private domain easily and laid her gently down on her bed. Then he sat down next to her. 'How are you feeling?' His eyes moved over the pallor of her skin and he reached out a hand towards her face.

She flinched nervously as his hand came into contact with her skin. 'Easy.' His voice was gently soothing as he turned her head to look at where she had hit the side of her forehead. 'You've got a nasty gash there.'

'That explains the headache.' She made an attempt at light humour but her voice trembled alarmingly.

'I'll get some warm water and bathe it for you.'

Before Holly had a chance to tell him there was no need for that he had disappeared out of the door. Holly leaned her head back against her pillows. What a nightmare; she still couldn't take it all in. How on earth had that fire started?

Quinlan came back with a bowl, some cotton wool and antiseptic. 'I've raided the bathroom cabinet.' He smiled at her as he sat back down on the edge of her bed.

Holly's heart started to pound heavily as she looked up at him. This was all wrong. Quinlan shouldn't be in her bedroom, sitting on the edge of her bed. How on earth had she managed to get herself into this predicament?

'Just turn your head again.' He gently caught her chin and moved her so that he could see the side of her face more clearly. Then, very gently, he started to bathe it. Holly didn't know what bothered her more, the touch of his hand or the warm water against her broken skin. She flinched away.

'Be a brave girl.' He spoke softly as he continued to clean around the area, and strangely enough she felt herself calm down a little.

'Is it bleeding?'

'Not really, but it looks nasty.' He finished and then put the antiseptic cream on. After the initial stinging it felt much better.

'Thanks.' She stared up at him with eyes that looked too big in the pallor of her face. 'It was you who brought me out of there, wasn't it?' she asked huskily.

He grinned. 'I was the only one around at the time,' he said lightly.

'Thank you, Quinlan,' she said softly. 'I owe you my life.'

'No need to go overboard.' One dark eyebrow lifted sardonically. 'I think you're still in shock, and they do say the best thing for that is hot sweet tea.'

Holly grimaced. 'I hate sugar in tea.'

'Well, you're just going to have to suffer it.' He stood up. 'In the circumstances you're very lucky that that's all you've got to suffer. Third-degree burns are no joke.'

She swallowed hard. She knew he was right. She could so easily have perished in that fire, or been very badly hurt. The thought made her feel sick inside.

'I'll get that tea.' He left her alone and she closed her aching eyes.

Quinlan had played it down but he had risked his life for her. The knowledge did strange things to her pulse-rate. She would never have expected Quin to follow her into that raging inferno. If someone had told her last week that Quinlan Montgomery would risk his life to save her, then sit on the edge of her bed, she would have laughed scornfully.

He came back into the room carrying the china cup and saucer. 'One cup of hot sweet tea.' He placed it down next to her. 'How's your throat?'

'A little rough,' she admitted, struggling to sit up against the pillows.

He reached down and put his hands around her to help her up. The touch of his fingers seemed to burn through the cotton nightshirt, making her suddenly very aware of her naked body beneath the thin clothing.

'Thanks.' She hoped her face wasn't as flushed as it felt as she looked up at him.

His firm lips slanted in an amused smile.

'Have I said something funny?' she asked, instantly on the defensive.

'Not at all. I'm just not used to this new Holly Fitzgerald; it's a novelty hearing you thank me all the time,' he said with a laugh.

She frowned. 'Well, enjoy it while you can. I'm sure I'll revert to my old self once the shock has worn off.' She was half serious, half joking.

He smiled, but it was a gentle smile. 'I hope so,' he said quietly.

The tone of his voice made her heart miss a beat. Disconcerted, she reached for the tea. It tasted horrible but she finished it, more for something to do to cover the awkwardness of the moment than anything else.

'It seems that the Fitzgeralds are in your debt,' she said lightly as she leaned her head back against the pillows. 'First of all you come to Flynn's aid, and now mine...' She trailed off as her throat started to ache furiously.

'Don't talk any more.' His voice sounded slightly strained, and she wondered if the smoke had caught his throat as well. Then he smiled at her and reached to take the empty cup from her. 'I'm just glad that I was here,' he said softly.

She gazed up into those intense eyes and felt her heart starting to pound uncomfortably. 'I'm glad that you were here as well,' she whispered huskily.

Flynn came in, shattering the strangely unreal moment. 'Holly, thank God.' The relief in her brother's voice was so deep it was almost tangible. 'I nearly had heart failure when I drove into the yard and saw the fire engine. Are you all right?'

'I'm fine,' she murmured. 'Where have you been? I was worried about you.'

'I bumped into Sinead at the pub and we decided to go into Dublin to a nightclub. I'm sorry, Holly—I should have been here.' He raked a hand through his hair in a distraught manner.

'It's all right, Flynn.' Holly shook her head. 'Perhaps it's just as well you weren't.'

'What happened?' he asked anxiously. 'Your voice sounds really weird.'

'Smoke,' Quinlan put in quietly. 'Holly took it upon herself to rescue the horses.'

Flynn shook his head in disbelief. 'I should have been here,' he muttered again.

'It's all right, Flynn...really.' Suddenly her eyes felt heavy. And it just seemed like too much effort even to talk.

'I think you should rest now, Holly,' Quinlan said quietly. She felt his hands against her waist as he pulled her slender body down so that her head was resting back against the pillows. Then he pulled the covers up and around her.

'I'm all right...really I...' Her voice trailed off as her head moved sideways against the comforting softness of her pillows. Vaguely she could hear the men's voices through what seemed like thick mists of sleepiness.

'I don't know how I'll ever repay you, Quinlan,' she could hear her brother saying just before they closed the door.

'Don't worry.' Quin's voice was sardonically dry. 'I'll think of something. Just make sure you call a doctor out to Holly in the morning.'

Holly frowned, and tried very hard to wake up, but she was fighting a losing battle and the conversation was lost as the mist completely enveloped her.

'Imagine Quinlan rescuing you like that!' Sinead's voice lifted with excitement.

'It wasn't that thrilling, I can assure you,' Holly muttered. Her throat still sounded husky even though it was four days since the awful incident. 'It was terrifying.'

Sinead nodded. 'I can see that by just looking out there.' She nodded towards the window and Holly didn't need to follow her glance out of the lounge windows to know that she was referring to the awful state of the stables. She had spent a lot of her spare moments recently just staring out at that building and marvelling that anything had got out of there alive.

'How did it start, do you know?'

'The firemen seem to think it was a cigarette end,' Holly said dismally. 'Which means that Flynn might find it hard to claim from the insurance people.'

Sinead made a face. 'That's really going to please him.'

'It's just one more reason for him to feel dissatisfied with the farm. He was talking about Australia again this morning,' Holly murmured sadly.

'I'm sure it's just talk and nothing more,' Sinead said firmly. 'Those are beautiful flowers.' She changed the subject abruptly and turned her attention towards the magnificent bouquet of flowers on the coffee-table.

'Yes.' Holly's eyes played contemplatively over the red roses. When she looked back at her friend she found that she was grinning at her.

'Well?' Sinead said with an imp of mischief in her bright eyes. 'Are you going to put me out of my misery? Are they or are they not from the gorgeous Quinlan?'

Holly hesitated for a moment. 'Well...yes... but——'

Sinead's laughter cut her off in mid-sentence. 'I knew it...I knew you two really had a soft spot for each other.'

'That is simply not true, Sinead.' Holly's tone was outraged. 'The flowers were just a get-well message.'

'Since when have red roses been a get-well message?' Sinead said scornfully.

Holly shook her head. 'You're getting it all out of proportion. I haven't even seen Quinlan since the night of the fire.'

'Well, you've only just got up out of bed,' Sinead said with a grin.

'Sinead, stop it,' Holly said firmly. 'There is nothing between Quin and me.'

'OK, OK. I won't say another word.' Sinead laughed. 'Except that Ross will be devastated. He's always liked you.'

'Sinead!' Holly frowned at her friend. 'Now change the subject. How are things with you? I believe that you had a wonderful night out with Flynn?'

'Now who's getting everything out of proportion?' Sinead said with a laugh, then admitted grudgingly, 'Yes, we did have a nice time.'

'Well, that night out did seem to cheer him up for a while, and he's actually working on the farm full-time again. Maybe you're right and Australia is just a passing fancy.'

'Yes.' Sinead looked away from her friend and for a moment Holly thought she saw a strange expression on her face.

'Sinead... is everything all right?'

'Of course.' Sinead still avoided her gaze and then her face brightened. 'You have a visitor,' she said, nodding towards the window.

'Oh, who?' Holly turned and her heart started to do strange somersaults when she saw the dark outline of Quinlan as he walked towards the front door.

'I'll let him in.' Before Holly could say anything Sinead had leapt to her feet and was racing towards the door.

It was silly to feel so nervous, but Holly felt completely on edge as she waited for Sinead to show him in. She didn't know what she should say to him. She owed him so much. Then there was this part of her that wished she had taken a little more care with her appearance today. She felt ordinary in the pale blue summer dress. It was a completely ridiculous thought; why on earth should she care what she was dressed in? It was only Quinlan. He usually saw her dressed in jeans anyway.

'Hello, Holly.' He strolled casually in, looking so attractive that for a moment she felt as if all her senses were on red alert.

'Hello, Quin.' Her voice was soft and husky.

'You've still got that incredibly sexy voice, I hear.' He grinned at her.

'You mean my smoke-inflamed tonsils,' she said, trying very hard to reduce the tension inside her with a joke.

He smiled. 'For a woman just recovering from a nasty shock, you look wonderful.'

Holly's cheeks flamed at that compliment, especially as Sinead had just walked in in time to hear it.

Her friend grinned. 'You've also got another male visitor,' she said softly.

Holly glanced around to see that Jamie had come with his dad, a bunch of wild flowers clutched in his little hands.

'For you, Holly. I hope you're feeling better.' He held them out very seriously as if he had been practising the speech that went with the flowers all day.

'Thank you, Jamie,' Holly was delighted to see the little boy. 'Do I get a kiss to go with the beautiful gift?'

The child nodded and stretched upwards to plant a kiss on the side of her cheek.

'So how are you feeling?' Quinlan asked, sitting down in the chair opposite.

'Much better, thank you.' It was strange how glad she felt to see him. She bit down on the softness of her lower lip. The smoke must have affected more than her throat, she thought wryly.

Sinead leaned against the side of the settee and smiled down at Quinlan. 'Shall I get you a cup of tea, Quin?' she offered.

He shook his head. 'No, thanks, Sinead. I'm not staying. Jamie and I have just dropped in on our way past. I'm taking him for a picnic out to Brittas Bay.'

'Is the lovely Fiona not accompanying you?' Sinead asked with a gleam of amusement in her voice.

'She's had to go into Dublin. There are a few things she wants to pick up from her house,' Quin answered easily.

'So she's planning on staying for some time, then?' Sinead continued.

'Until Jamie goes back to school, anyway.' Quin's voice was relaxed but Holly wondered if he was getting fed up with people asking him that question, with that same speculative edge to it. Was there anything going on between Quinlan and Fiona?

He glanced across at Holly and smiled. It was a smile that did strange things to Holly's pulse-rate.

'Thank you for the flowers,' she murmured, trying desperately to pull her scattered wits together.

'I'm glad you liked them.' His eyes held hers for a moment too long and she looked away, flustered.

'Well, I'll get off now and leave you to talk in peace,' Sinead said with a smile as she reached for her handbag.

'Oh... don't go, Sinead,' Holly said hastily. Even though Quinlan had Jamie with him she felt nervous about being left with him for some reason.

'I have to. I've got to get back to the shop; Saturday is a busy day for us.'

'The health business booming, is it?' Quinlan asked with a smile.

'Not bad. I think people are turning more to natural remedies these days.'

'Well, I'm certainly grateful for the stuff you brought for my throat, Sinead,' Holly said as she stood up to walk with her friend to the door.

'What you need is to relax for a while. You've been overworking on the farm,' Sinead said with a smile. 'For instance, it's a beautiful sunny day; you should go somewhere and enjoy it. That's the best kind of natural remedy.'

Holly's face flamed at her friend's words. She knew very well that Sinead was hinting that she should go with Quinlan and Jamie on their picnic. 'I've had enough relaxation these last few days,' she said quickly. 'In fact, I'm looking forward to getting back to work.'

'All the same, Sinead is right,' Quinlan put in smoothly. 'It is a beautiful day. Why don't you come out with Jamie and me?'

'That's very nice of you, Quin, but——'

'No buts,' Quin cut across her firmly. 'Jamie and I insist.'

'Yes, we do,' the little boy put in, with such a solemn look on his face that Holly had to smile.

'Well, now that's settled I'll be on my way,' Sinead said with a laugh.

'I'll let you out.' Holly followed her friend into the hallway. 'What on earth made you say that?' she said in a hoarse whisper.

'What?' Sinead turned wide, innocent eyes on her friend and then grinned. 'Oh, hell, it's a beautiful day, Holly, and he is a gorgeous hunk of a man. If I had the chance to spend the afternoon with him I'd be off like a shot.'

'Shh!' Nervously Holly glanced back towards the lounge. She didn't want Quinlan hearing.

Sinead laughed happily as she went out through the front door. 'Bye, Holly,' she said in a loud voice. 'Have a wonderful afternoon, and don't do anything I wouldn't.'

Holly felt most embarrassed as she turned to go back in to Quinlan. He would have heard that, of course. Really, Sinead was too much sometimes.

Quinlan grinned at her as she went back into the lounge. 'I think that leaves us with plenty of scope,' he said with a wicked gleam in his blue eyes.

Holly's heart thudded wildly and she could feel herself growing even hotter. 'Pay no attention to Sinead,' she said crisply. 'Her sense of humour sometimes extends to the ridiculous.'

Quinlan merely smiled at that. 'Run and get your bikini,' he said. 'And, at the risk of extending towards the ridiculous, make it a brief one. It's a very hot day out there and getting hotter by the minute.'

He was teasing her, of course. Quinlan seemed to like nothing better than to get her flustered. 'If it's that hot we'll have to find some shade. I can't take too much sun,' she told him promptly. 'And I don't possess anything that brief.'

'Pity,' he drawled, and then laughed as he succeeded in making her blush. 'Don't worry, Holly. I'll keep every inch of that beautiful skin of yours perfectly protected.'

Holly turned to get her swimming costume, her nerves racing in utter turmoil. She should never have agreed to this, she thought as she slowly went up to her bedroom. Quinlan might have saved her life but she was risking her neck going anywhere with the man. He was trouble, she just knew he was.

Despite the feeling of doom, the day turned out to be very enjoyable. Jamie chatted happily in the back of the car all the way there so that Holly was saved from having to make small talk with Quinlan. The child's enthusiasm and excitement over the trip to the beach was infectious, and Holly found herself getting quite caught up in it, so much so that she found herself cheering with Jamie when the sand dunes leading to the beautiful golden beach came into view.

Quinlan caught her eye and smiled. It was a strangely tender smile, Holly thought for a moment, and then she shook her head. No, she was definitely going crazy...how could she possibly mistake one of Quinlan's sardonic looks for something tender? Maybe the heat was getting to her?

Quin parked the car and then opened the boot to get out a picnic hamper and a large travelling rug.

'You've thought of everything,' Holly murmured as he also reached in and got out a large parasol for the sun.

'I told you I'd look after that beautiful skin of yours,' he grinned. 'You've risked burning to a crisp once before. So I don't think we should take any more chances.' He picked up a large tube of sun-cream and put it into her hand.

She glanced down at it and frowned. It was a very high protection factor for delicate skin. 'Anyone would think you had been expecting me to come with you today.'

'Of course not. I didn't even think of asking you until Sinead suggested it.' There was a touch of dry humour in his voice.

'Oh!' Now Holly really felt foolish. Of course Quinlan hadn't planned to invite her. He probably had been hoping for a relaxing time alone with his son this afternoon, when Sinead had more or less forced him into being polite and inviting her along. She fell silent, strangely upset by the idea.

Brittas Bay was an area of unspoilt natural beauty. The turquoise-blue of the Irish Sea swept into the golden sands that reached for miles along the coast. Tall sand dunes flanked the flat gold of the sand, coarse grass stirring every now and then as a slight breeze ruffled the sharp green blades.

Jamie caught hold of Holly's hand as they started to walk over the dunes. 'Can you swim, Holly?' he asked with a proud tilt to his head. 'I can. My dad taught me.'

'That's very good, Jamie. I'm afraid I'm not a very confident swimmer but I just about manage.'

'Perhaps you need some lessons,' Quin remarked in that deep velvet-smooth voice that made Holly's pulse-rate seem to shoot madly up. 'A good teacher can make all the difference.'

'You... you're probably right.' Holly tried very hard to keep her voice cool and steady. What on earth was the matter with her? she thought frantically. Why did she suddenly imagine that everything he said to her had some kind of a double meaning? The man was probably just making polite conversation.

They found a spot down near the edge of the sand dunes and Quinlan spread the large blanket on the ground and arranged the parasol so that Holly could lie with her face in the shade if she wanted.

'Thank you.' Holly sat down and glanced across at the blue of the sea. 'It's so beautiful here,' she murmured reflectively. 'I used to come here sometimes on school trips and once or twice with my parents during the school holidays.'

'So did I.' Quinlan smiled over at her. 'We've had a very similar upbringing; we're members of the same small community yet we hardly know each other.'

'Well, that's hardly surprising,' she murmured.

'Seeing that our parents didn't speak, you mean?' He shot an amused glance down at her.

'I didn't mean that... I meant that there are several years between us. We had different sets of friends,' she said, feeling uncomfortable with this subject.

'Our paths crossed quite a few times,' he continued. 'I can think of a lot of parties that we were both invited to.' He grinned at her. 'You always used to stick your nose in the air when you saw me. I think you enjoyed ignoring me.'

She shook her head. 'That's your imagination. I hardly noticed you.' It was a blatant lie. Holly had never failed to notice Quinlan. He wasn't the type of man you could overlook. He had always been devastatingly attractive, always the centre of female attention.

He laughed, but thankfully he didn't follow that up. Instead he stood and pulled the pale blue shirt over his head. His bronzed muscles seem to gleam in the sunshine and his skin looked incredibly smooth, Holly thought, her eyes watching his every movement with a kind of dreamy fascination. It was only when his fingers reached to take off the beige chinos that she hurriedly averted her eyes.

'Are you not going to get into your swimsuit?' Quinlan asked in an amused tone.

'Er... yes.' Holly stood up, grateful that she had had the foresight to put her swimming costume on under her clothes. She pulled the blue dress up over her head and shook her long auburn hair back as the dress disturbed it. Unaware that Quinlan was watching her, she sat back down and stretched her long legs into the sunshine.

The costume she wore was high-legged and showed her curvy figure to its best advantage, the bright green colour complementing the glow of her auburn hair, the dark colour of her eyes.

'So are we friends now?' Quinlan sat down beside her. The intimate tone of his voice made her heart start to race.

'I suppose so.' She didn't look up at him, but traced her fingers through the sand, her eyes following the sifting grains as if they were of utmost importance.

'Holly?' He caught hold of that hand, forcing her eyes to lift to his. '"I suppose so" isn't much of an answer.' The blue eyes were sharply probing as they held hers.

'I wouldn't be a very nice person if I didn't consider you a friend after what you did for me,' she murmured softly.

'If you are talking about my getting you out of those stables, then I'd rather that wasn't a factor in this,' he said seriously. 'I'd have done that for anybody.'

She swallowed hard. 'But you did it for me, Quinlan... I do owe you a lot.'

He shook his head. 'You don't owe me anything.' His voice was gravel-rough for a moment, as if he was angry.

She frowned, not understanding the vehemence in his tone. 'Quin, I am grateful. If it hadn't been for your saving me I might not be here now.'

'I'd say that was a pretty accurate statement,' he grated sardonically, then turned away from her. For a moment there was silence as he watched his son.

Jamie was making sandcastles a few feet away, his young face concentrating earnestly on the job.

'Come on, Jamie.' Quinlan stood up suddenly. 'Let's go for a swim.'

The child immediately left what he had been doing. 'Are you coming, Holly?' he asked excitedly.

Holly glanced up at Quinlan uncertainly. His mood seemed to have changed. One moment he had been laughing and joking with her, the next he was abruptly angry.

He stared down at her and his blue eyes seemed hard and uncompromising.

'Er...no, Jamie, I'll stay and look after the clothes and things.'

The child nodded and then took hold of his father's hand as they walked away down towards the sea.

Holly watched them go. Jamie was skipping happily alongside his father. Quinlan was smiling down at him and talking with him and the child was happily chatting back. Quinlan looked so big and powerful next to his son, yet he seemed infinitely gentle with him. As Holly watched, he picked the child up and sat him on his shoulders and then ran towards the blue of the sea. The gentle breeze carried snatches of the child's laughter back to Holly, and she smiled to herself as she lay back and closed her eyes.

Jamie was motherless, but his father certainly loved and cherished him. For a moment she found herself thinking about Camilla Montgomery. She had seen her several times. It was hard to live in a small community and not bump into people.

She had been extremely beautiful and very sophisticated. In a way, Fiona looked a lot like her sister. Camilla had had cool, classical looks. She had been a tall, willowy blonde who always dressed in the latest designer clothes. Considering that she had lived on a farm, Holly had never seen her dressed in jeans. But then Camilla and

Fiona were city girls. Both had been brought up in Dublin.

It had been no surprise to anyone when Quinlan had married Camilla. Their parents had been close friends and Quinlan had dated Camilla a lot over the years. They had been obviously very much in love.

They had been married for just over a year when Camilla gave birth to Jamie. Then, tragically, just one year later she had died. Her death had filled the small community with sadness. She had been so young, so vibrant and she had had so much to live for.

Holly remembered bumping into Quinlan just after her death. He had looked so gaunt and sad that it had torn at her heart and she had stopped to offer her condolences.

'Thanks, Holly.' A ghost of a smile had lit his features for a moment as his eyes moved over her face.

Holly had shrugged then, feeling suddenly self-conscious. 'She seemed a nice girl,' she'd said simply.

Quinlan had nodded. Then, much to Holly's relief, they had been interrupted by someone else who wanted to speak to him and she had been able to escape.

The incident had stayed in Holly's mind for a long time afterwards. It was the first time that she had spoken to Quinlan of her own volition and his grief had struck a deep chord of sympathy inside her. As bad as she had thought him, no one deserved such an awful stroke of fate.

'Are you asleep?' Quin's voice startled her and her eyes flew open.

'No...no, I was miles away, though.' She sat up and smiled at him. 'Did you enjoy your swim?'

'Yes, it's quite warm.' He reached for a towel and wiped the glistening beads of water from his tanned, lithe body before sitting down on the rug.

'Where's Jamie?' Holly shaded her eyes and looked around.

'He's found himself a little girlfriend.' Quin grinned at her and then pointed down the sand a little way.

Holly followed his gaze and saw Jamie playing ball with a little three-year-old.

'Hopefully he'll tire himself out and we'll get a few minutes' peace going home in the car,' Quinlan said with a smile.

Holly smiled back at him, glad that his mood seemed cheerful again. Maybe she had just imagined his coolness before.

He opened the picnic hamper. 'In the meantime, I think we should have a glass of champagne.'

'Champagne?' Holly frowned and glanced over at the contents of the hamper. Sure enough, there was a big bottle of champagne nestling in a cooling unit. Next to it were two glasses and a wondrous selection of food. 'And two glasses, I see.' She looked back up at him and he smiled.

'Well, I live in hope. I thought, if I packed two glasses and some good champagne, surely fate would smile down and provide me with a lovely companion to share it with.'

She grinned, suddenly happy at the thought that he *had* planned all along to invite her this afternoon. Then she shook her head. 'But unfortunately fate forgot that I don't drink.'

'Surely you'll have a drink of champagne? We have a lot to celebrate.' He lifted it out and popped the cork easily, pouring the sparkling liquid straight into the delicate crystal flute. 'I'll put some orange juice in it for you if you like.' As he spoke he was already pouring the juice into the glass.

Holly smiled at him and accepted the glass. 'Thank you.' She lifted the glass towards his. 'But just what are we celebrating?'

'Our friendship, of course.' He lifted his glass and it clinked gently against the crystal of hers. 'The end of the Fitzgerald-Montgomery feud.'

For a moment their eyes met and then Holly glanced away. Her hand trembled slightly as she lifted the glass to her lips.

The rest of the afternoon passed very pleasurably. They ate lunch and Holly finished a few more glasses of Buck's Fizz. Then they played at building sandcastles with Jamie, much to his delight.

Holly was quite sorry when the day came to an end and they packed everything up to come home. As Quinlan had predicted, Jamie fell asleep in the back of the car when they had been travelling for a while.

Holly glanced around at the sleeping little boy and smiled. He looked so cute, his cheeks bright from the fresh air, his dark hair tousled from the sea breeze.

'I think Jamie enjoyed his day out,' she said as she turned back to the road ahead.

'He thinks you're wonderful,' Quinlan said with a smile.

'Does he?' Holly felt a little embarrassed by the compliment. 'Well, the feeling is mutual. You have a lovely son, Quinlan.'

'I know.' For a moment his voice sounded wistful. 'I just wish sometimes that Jamie had a mother. It's hard for him.'

Holly swallowed hard and glanced at Quinlan's rugged features as he concentrated on the road ahead. For a moment her heart went out to him. He had been so devastated when Camilla had died. 'It must be hard for you as well,' she said softly. 'It's not easy bringing up a child on your own.'

'No, it's not,' he agreed easily, then smiled at her. 'But I am considering marrying again.'

For a moment Holly's stomach seemed to plunge in a wild, crazy way as if someone had just pushed her from the top of a multi-storey building. 'I see.' It was all she could think of to say. Her mind whirled. Who was he thinking of marrying? The only person who sprang to mind was Fiona.

Quinlan turned the car through the gates of the Fitzgerald farm. It was starting to get dark now and the windows of the farmhouse threw out a welcoming golden light up ahead.

'Flynn will be wondering where I've got to,' Holly murmured. She could hardly wait to get out of the car now and away from Quin. It was strange that she should feel like that so suddenly when she had so much enjoyed the day.

'Tell Flynn that I'll be over to see him in the morning,' Quin said as he pulled the car to a standstill outside the front door.

For once Holly didn't ask any questions. 'All right.' She nodded. 'Thanks for a lovely day out, Quinlan.' She reached for the door-handle.

'You're very welcome.' He leaned across towards her and suddenly her heart stood still.

His hand brushed the hair back from her forehead gently. 'I'm glad you're feeling better.'

She didn't know what to say. He seemed so close to her. She could look deep into those blue eyes and nearly drown in their beauty.

His hand moved and suddenly his finger was delicately tracing the line of her lower lip. 'Goodnight, then.' His head came even closer and he kissed her lips lightly.

Holly's heart thudded wildly. She knew he was just being friendly, that it was no more than a goodnight kiss, but it did very strange things to her body. She felt hot inside and her lips tingled so alarmingly that she longed to put a hand up to them to try and wipe away the sensation.

'Goodnight, Quinlan.' Her voice was a mere husky whisper as she tried very hard to gather herself together.

She had a fleeting glimpse of his smile before she turned and got out. She didn't wait for him to drive off but went directly inside.

Her lips were still burning from the gentle touch of his mouth and she gave in to the temptation to rub her hand over them, but the sensation for some reason persisted.

'Holly, is that you?' Flynn called to her from the lounge.

'Yes, I'm coming.' With a determined effort to collect herself she went in to him.

The first thing her eyes went to when she opened the lounge door was the portrait of Lucinda Fitzgerald. The girl seemed to be smiling down at her with a wistful look in her eyes. For one strange moment Holly had a feeling that something was about to happen, something that would change her life forever.

'Where have you been?'

She blinked and looked away from the painting towards her brother. What on earth was the matter with her? 'I...I went to Brittas with Quinlan and Jamie for a picnic.'

'Really?' Flynn stood up, and there was a look on his face of sheer relief.

She frowned. 'It was just a spur-of-the-moment thing.'

'Yes. I'm glad.'

Why did he look so pleased? Holly shook her head in complete puzzlement. 'Quin says he will be over in the morning to see you.'

'Good.' Flynn stretched and raked a hand through his dark hair. 'Do me a favour, Holly, will you? Make me something to eat. I've just finished work and I've still got some paperwork to see to.'

Holly nodded. 'Yes, all right.' She hesitated in the doorway for a moment. 'What paperwork?'

'I'll tell you later.' Flynn turned towards the bureau in the corner.

With a frown Holly turned to do as he had asked. Obviously Flynn had a lot on his mind and he wasn't about to talk about it tonight.

As she went through into the kitchen her mind turned towards Quinlan. Who was he thinking of marrying... Fiona? It seemed the most likely possibility; after all, she had moved into Montgomery House with him.

Were they sleeping together? The question sprang unbidden into her mind and, very angry with herself, she started to work. She didn't give a damn what the arrangement between Fiona and Quinlan consisted of. It was none of her business.

Why was it, then, that she could think of nothing else? Why was it when she got into bed that night the only thing on her mind was that Quinlan was getting married?

CHAPTER SIX

HOLLY was up early the next day. She hadn't slept too well that night and she was anxious to get back to work.

It was another beautiful morning, the sun rising in a glorious red ball of fire over the fields.

She had a quick cup of tea and was on her way out to saddle Becky when she heard a car driving up outside. Then she heard Flynn talking to someone in a low voice. She frowned. Surely it wouldn't be Quin? She had hoped to be out by the time he arrived. For some reason she really didn't want to see him again for a while.

Taking a deep breath, she made herself open the kitchen door and stroll out into the yard to see who their visitor was.

Her whole body relaxed immediately when she saw that it was Ross, who was leaning back against the door of his Land Rover.

'Holly, how are you?' He grinned over at her and raked a hand in a rather self-conscious way through his sandy-coloured hair.

'I'm much better, thank you, Ross.'

'You can ask her yourself now, Ross,' Flynn put in with a smile over at Holly.

'Ask me what?' Holly's glance moved from her brother back to Ross who to her surprise started to look a little uncomfortable.

'Well, I was just wondering if you would like to come out to dinner with me tonight.' He shrugged. 'If you don't feel up to it, though, I'll understand.'

'That would be lovely,' Holly answered immediately, the thought of a relaxing evening in his pleasant company appealing instantly to her jangled nerves.

'Right, then.' His smile brightened considerably. 'I'll pick you up about eight.'

She nodded.

'While you're here, Ross, perhaps you'd take a look at my horse,' Flynn interrupted the conversation. 'He cut himself as he came out of the stables the night of the fire. I thought it was healing all right but I'm not so sure now.'

'Of course I'll look at him.' Ross reached back into his car for his bag and together they walked towards the lower field.

Holly sat on the fence and watched as Flynn tried to catch the animal for Ross. She laughed at the frisky antics of the stallion as he refused to stand still for a moment.

'I don't think there's too much wrong with him.' Ross smiled as Flynn finally got hold of him.

Becky came over and stood next to Holly as she watched the men. Holly reached out and stroked the animal's soft nose and she nuzzled closer, looking for the sugar lump Holly usually had for her.

Holly was so engrossed in listening to the men's conversation that she didn't hear anyone coming up behind her. When the deep, familiar male voice spoke close to her ear, she nearly fell off the fence.

'Careful.' Strong arms reached out and grabbed her around the waist. The touch of his hands on her body made her heart thud wildly.

'Quin! You startled me.' She tried to break away from him and slide off the fence but he held her firmly and his lips brushed the softness of her hair as he spoke.

'This is the second time I've had to rescue you dramatically.' He smiled. 'You should be more careful.'

'Hello, Quin.' Ross looked over and his eyes seemed to take in the closeness of their stance with a look of surprise.

'Morning, Ross, Flynn.' Quin nodded at them, but he made no attempt to let Holly go. 'Trouble with the stallion?'

'No.' Ross shook his head. 'It's just a superficial wound. I'll give you some cream for it, Flynn.' Ross bent down and picked up his bag and then walked over towards them.

Holly put her hands over Quin's and pulled them away from her waist so that she could climb down from the fence.

'You're bright and early this morning,' she said, brushing her auburn hair away from her face to try and restore it to some kind of order. Then she looked up at him with what she hoped was a very composed air.

He grinned. 'Well, I've got a busy day ahead. Got to make up for all the work I missed yesterday.'

Somehow there seemed to be a warm, intimate note to his voice as he spoke, as if they had shared more than just a picnic yesterday.

'Yes, I believe you had a good time,' Flynn remarked, coming over to join them. 'It's a long time since I went down to Brittas Bay.'

'Perhaps you should take Sinead, while we're still having this glorious weather,' Ross remarked with a smile.

'Do you think she would come?' Flynn asked.

'Well, you persuaded her to go for a night out on the town with you.' Ross laughed. 'So I would say your chances looked good.' Then he glanced at his watch. 'I'd better get off. I have a lot of calls to make.'

They all walked back towards the house together.

'So I'll pick you up at eight tonight,' Ross said in a quiet voice to Holly as they stopped by his car.

'Where are you going this evening?' Quinlan asked, before Holly had a chance to say anything.

'Just for a quiet meal,' Ross shrugged. 'I haven't booked anything yet.'

'I see.' For a moment Quin's eyes rested on Holly. She tried to hold his gaze without flinching but she felt most uncomfortable. How was it that Quin was able to make her feel so on edge just with a mere look?

'In that case, why don't the two of you come up to the house and have dinner with Fiona and me tonight?' Quin continued smoothly.

Holly could feel herself growing hot at the very thought. There was no way she wanted to dine at Montgomery House with Quin and Fiona. It made her squirm just to think about it.

'Well, that's very nice of you, Quin,' Ross started. 'But we wouldn't like to put you to that trouble.'

Holly heaved a silent breath of relief.

'It's no trouble at all. Mary, my cook, will see to it all.' Quinlan smiled at Holly. 'So what do you say, Holly? Shall I expect you at eight?'

Holly's mind raced wildly for a polite way of refusing, but nothing sprang to her confused mind so she ended up smiling and saying, 'That would be lovely, thank you, Quin.'

Quinlan's lips curved in an almost mocking smile for a moment. Then he looked away from her and over towards Flynn. 'You're welcome as well, Flynn... and Sinead.'

'Thanks, Quin, but I'll have to pass. I've already made other plans for this evening.'

'Another time, then,' Quin said easily.

'Well, I'll get off.' Ross opened the door of his car and slung his bag in the back. 'I'll pick you up about quarter to eight, Holly.'

She nodded and watched as he started the engine and drove off.

'Well, shall we get down to business, Flynn?' Quinlan asked smoothly.

'Right you are.' Flynn turned to lead the way back into the house.

Holly watched them go with a frown. What on earth were they discussing?

'See you later, Holly,' Quin said with a lazy smile in her direction.

'I suppose so,' Holly murmured drily. For a moment she just stood there. She felt as if Quinlan was manipulating them all in some way. He had very easily changed her plans for the evening... now he was doing some kind of deal with Flynn. For some reason it all made her feel helpless. As if Quinlan was taking over all their lives in some way.

The sound of Becky neighing down by the gate brought her back to reality and with a shrug she went to get her saddle from one of the out-houses. She was being silly, she told herself crisply. Her brother could deal with Quinlan and she could certainly hold her own around him. There was no way that Quinlan Montgomery could take over their lives... it was a foolish thought.

That confidence seemed to diminish as the day wore on. By the time she went upstairs to start getting ready for the evening ahead she was feeling far from self-assured about Quinlan.

She spent twenty minutes studying the contents of her wardrobe. She hadn't a clue what to wear, even though her mind had turned to the problem several times during the day. In the end she selected a pale blue suit. The skirt was short but the jacket came down below her hips. She teamed it with a soft white blouse and selected a string of pears to decorate the creamy expanse of her throat. Then she went to have a shower.

She was ready just in time. She was just flicking a brush through the long length of her hair and putting on an extra dash of her favourite perfume when the doorbell went.

'You look fabulous!' Ross enthused immediately.

'Thank you.' She smiled at him. He looked very handsome in a dark grey suit, a silver-blue tie adding a gleam of colour to the outfit.

'I am ready; I'll just get my handbag.' She picked it up from the lounge table and then followed him out to his car.

'I'm rather disappointed, to tell you the truth,' Ross said once they had set off down the drive.

'Disappointed?' She glanced at him curiously.

'I had hoped to have you to myself this evening,' he said, glancing away from the road for just a moment.

'Oh...' For a second Holly hesitated. She was unsure how to take that. Ross had always been just a friend, yet by the sudden intimate tone of his voice she half wondered if the night out had meant more to him. 'Well... I'm sure we'll have a nice time anyway.' She decided to make light of his words and pretend that she was looking forward to dining with the others. She had no wish to give Ross the false idea that tonight was anything other than a casual date for her.

'Yes, I suppose so.' He sounded upset for a moment.

'What's Sinead doing tonight?' Deliberately Holly changed the subject.

'No idea. I haven't seen her for a while,' Ross murmured, obviously not pleased with the change in the conversation.

They turned in through the entrance gates of Quin's house. It was a moment before the large imposing residence came into view.

'Beautiful house,' Holly remarked idly as she saw it again.

The sun was starting to set now and it gleamed over the soft red brick and the green ivy, making it shine as if someone were shining a spotlight down on it, highlighting it like a jewel among the colour of the well laid-out gardens.

'Yes, it is,' Ross agreed. 'I believe it was built by Quin's great-great-great-grandfather. The family has always been very wealthy. Of course Quin has added greatly to the family fortune. His stud farm alone must bring in a fortune. He's had a lot of successful racehorses over the last few years.'

Holly glanced at Ross as she detected a dry note in his voice. 'I thought you liked Quin?' she asked softly. 'You sound almost...envious.'

Ross brought the car to a halt outside the house and smiled over at her. 'I suppose I am,' he said in a low tone. 'But not of his wealth or success. I'm jealous of the fact that he's managed to captivate you. To me that's far more precious than all the money in the world.'

Holly shook her head. 'Ross, I don't know what you mean. Quin has not "captivated me", as you put it.' She frowned. 'I've only just started speaking to the man, for heaven's sake!'

'But you've always had a thing for him,' Ross continued firmly. 'When Quin enters a room you have eyes for no one else.'

'What utter rubbish!' Holly reached for the door-handle and climbed out into the warmth of the summer evening. Yet despite the warmth she was shaking. It was anger, she told herself crossly. Ross had no right to say such things. It was all utterly untrue.

Ross smiled at her as he came around and walked with her up the steps towards the front door. 'I'm sorry if I've upset you, Holly.' He pressed the front-door bell with a firm decisive kind of movement. 'But I couldn't fail to notice. To me it's very obvious that you're in love with the man.'

'Ross!' Holly's voice escaped in a kind of strangled gasp. She was utterly shocked that he should voice those words... and here on Quinlan's doorstep of all places!

The door swung open at that moment and she tried very hard to summon a polite smile as she looked up into the deep blue of Quinlan's eyes.

He looked incredibly handsome. He wore a dark suit that emphasised the powerful lines of his body, and a white silk shirt that contrasted starkly with the tanned skin and dark, dark hair. He smiled at her and for a brief moment she felt almost mesmerised by him.

It was true. She swallowed hard. She had always been in love with Quinlan Montgomery; the stark fact seemed so plain now, yet she had never realised it before. Not until Ross had so vividly spelt it out, and then she had looked at Quinlan as if for the first time, without all the old preconceived ideas from her childhood tangling up her thoughts.

'Come on in.' Quinlan stood back and they walked past him. 'Shall I take your jacket for you, Holly?'

'Thanks.' It was about as much as Holly could manage to say; she still felt as if she was in a state of dazed shock.

The light touch of his hands against her shoulder made her pulse race and her cheeks flare with a delicate tinge of colour.

The door to the lounge opened and Fiona came out, looking more glamorous than ever.

'I'm so glad you could both come,' she said with a smile.

It was as if she had issued the invitations, Holly thought drily. She had the distinct impression that Fiona Matthews was enjoying playing at being Quinlan's hostess. Or maybe she wasn't playing? Maybe Quinlan had already asked her to be his wife? The idea stole into her mind and hung heavily around her heart like a dull ache.

'Come on into the lounge. I think we have time for a pre-dinner drink before Mary calls us through to eat,' the woman continued silkily.

'Thank you.' Trying very hard to gather herself together, Holly walked into the lounge, closely followed by the others.

She sat down in one of the deep pale buttercup settees and watched as Fiona made a great show of organising all their drinks.

'Now, Holly, what would you like?' The woman opened the small drinks cabinet and stood poised with one hand hovering over the rows of crystal glasses.

'Just a glass of mineral water with a dash of lime if you have it,' Holly said politely.

'Really?' The woman frowned. 'Wouldn't you prefer a Dubonnet or even a sherry?'

'Holly doesn't really drink, Fiona,' Quinlan put in easily. He reached across and pulled out a bottle of Irish spring water. 'I think this is the one you like, isn't it, Holly?'

Holly nodded, faintly surprised that Quinlan knew exactly what she drank.

'Well, each to her own.' Fiona shrugged and poured the drink for her. Then she walked across to hand it to her.

She was wearing a very sophisticated black dress that clung to her voluptuous curves in a very seductive way. Her blonde hair was loose and looked as if it had been recently permed, because it now lay in a mass of golden curls around her shoulders. Her make-up as usual was perfect: red lips and smouldering dark eyes. For a moment Holly found herself thinking that it wasn't surprising that Quinlan had chosen her to be his wife. She was extremely attractive. And maybe even the fact that she was his late wife's sister had been a drawing point for him. She did look very like Camilla.

Ross had a Scotch and water with Quin while Fiona choose a dry Martini. Then they all sat down. Much to Holly's discomfort, Quinlan sat next to her on the settee, while Fiona sat next to Ross on the settee opposite.

'So how are you feeling now?' Fiona asked Holly. 'The fire must have been a terrible shock.'

'Yes.' Holly sipped her drink. 'But I'm feeling much better now and it's all due to Quin.'

'Really?' Quinlan turned amused eyes on her. 'You mean that champagne yesterday made all the difference?'

'I meant that I wouldn't even be alive if it hadn't been for you,' Holly said simply.

'Nonsense.' Quinlan dismissed that quickly. 'You don't know what would have happened.'

'Yes, I do,' Holly maintained firmly. 'I owe you a lot, Quin.'

He shrugged. 'I shall just have to find some way you can repay me,' he said with a glint in his eye.

'Pay no attention to Quin,' Fiona put in quickly. 'He's a terrible tease.'

'Talking of repayment, I still haven't paid you for the electric fence you put up,' Holly said seriously.

'Forget about it. Flynn and I have sorted all the business out.'

'What do you mean...sorted all the business out?' Holly frowned.

'Come on, you two,' Ross put in impatiently. 'We're supposed to be relaxing, not talking about business.'

'You're quite right,' Quinlan agreed easily. He lifted his glass to his lips and his eyes studied Holly over its rim. 'Business can wait until later,' he murmured.

Holly very much wanted to continue with the conversation but she bit down on her lip and tried just to relax and switch off about business, and about her feelings towards Quin.

A few minutes later Mary came and called them to go through to the dining-room.

Like all the rooms in Quinlan's house, the dining-room was elegantly decorated. The table was set with polished silver on an Irish linen tablecloth. Waterford glasses gleamed as candlelight flickered over the table, giving everything a very romantic look.

'You sit opposite me, Holly,' Quinlan said, holding out a chair for her so that she had no other choice but to sit facing him.

Fiona sat beside Quin, facing Ross.

'How do you like living in the country?' Ross asked Fiona after they had been served with their first course of pâté and hot buttered toast.

'It has its compensations.' Fiona cast a flirtatious glance at Quinlan. 'I miss Dublin, of course, but it's only an hour away. I'd say I've settled in very well...wouldn't you, Quin?' She turned towards him and batted long dark lashes as if she was waiting for his approval with a kind of breathless wonder.

'I suppose you have,' Quinlan said nonchalantly. 'I've certainly appreciated your help with Jamie over the summer holidays.'

'Jamie can be difficult,' Fiona said with a shrug. 'I have tried my best with the boy but, as I've said before, you should really think about sending him to boarding-school next year, Quinlan. It would do him the world of good.'

Quinlan shrugged in an offhand manner. 'We'll see.'

Holly felt her food starting to stick in her throat. Quinlan couldn't be serious about sending Jamie away to school. He was just a baby, and to Holly's way of thinking he needed his father to be around him.

Quinlan caught her expression across the table and smiled at her. 'What do you think about Jamie going away to school, Holly?' he asked suddenly.

Holly didn't hesitate. 'I think he's too young yet. I also think that the fact that he only has you and no mother makes him very vulnerable.' Holly leaned across towards him, unaware of how intensely bright her eyes were as she strove to convince him that she was right. 'He needs to see more of you, not less. He needs the security of knowing that you love him and are there for him.' She sat back in her chair as she finished, suddenly feeling self-conscious about the emotion in her voice.

Quinlan was watching her with a strange expression on his tough features. She couldn't quite work out what he was thinking. She hoped fervently that she hadn't just made a fool of herself, but she couldn't help it. She was very fond of Jamie and she just couldn't stand the thought of the little five-year-old being unhappy.

Quinlan lifted his wine glass to his lips, took a sip of its golden contents and just smiled at her.

'Well, I can't agree, Holly,' Fiona put in. 'The child needs discipline.'

Holly shrugged. 'Maybe. But he also needs love, and I just happen to think that's more important.'

Fiona's eyes glittered coolly as they rested on Holly's face. It was clear that she was not at all pleased with that statement. Holly didn't really care whether the woman was annoyed with her or not. She had spoken her mind, and at the end of the day it was up to Quinlan how he chose to bring up his son.

'I shall certainly bear your words in mind,' Quinlan said quietly.

The door opened and the young girl who had served their first course started to clear away the dishes and serve their main course, roast pheasant with a delicious accompaniment of fresh vegetables and new potatoes.

The conversation turned to lighter things. Ross spoke about his work as a vet. He was very amusing and he soon had everyone laughing about some of his more reluctant patients.

'It can be a dangerous job,' Quin remarked as Ross finished a story about a very angry bull who had chased him around his medical bag and out of his field.

'Well...' Ross hesitated. 'Animals can be unpredictable and, if they're in pain or frightened, sometimes their way of dealing with it is through anger.'

'A little bit like a woman,' Quin remarked drily, then grinned as he caught Holly's look of outrage. 'Well, don't deny it, Holly. You have verbally lashed out at me many a time. You're as unpredictable as a highly strung, frightened colt.'

'Quinlan, that is total rubbish! I am...' Holly trailed off as she saw the gleam in Quinlan's eye and realised that he was just teasing her to get a reaction. 'You are an utter torment, Quinlan,' she said with a shake of her head and a small laugh.

The conversation was interrupted as the dining-room door opened a couple of inches and Jamie peeped around it. 'Daddy, I can't sleep,' he said, rubbing his eyes in a tired way and then staring at the adults around the table in a bewildered way. He smiled as his eyes locked on Holly. 'Hello,' he said in a low voice.

'Hello, sweetheart. What's the matter?' Holly asked immediately.

'I don't feel very well.' He padded further into the room and came to stand beside her at the table. He was wearing a pair of blue striped pyjamas that looked as if they were a size too big for him. His dark hair was ruffled and his small face looked rosy-cheeked.

Fiona made an impatient sound. 'This is exactly what I mean,' she said with a sigh. 'The child is undisciplined.

There's no way he should be allowed to come downstairs after he has been put to bed.'

Ignoring Fiona's outburst, Holly placed a hand on the child's forehead. It was no wonder Jamie had rosy cheeks: he was burning up. 'He has a slight temperature,' she said, looking across at Quinlan.

Quinlan immediately got to his feet and came around to put his hand on Jamie's head. 'So you have,' he said, and picked the child up. 'Come on then, son, let's get you back into bed.'

Jamie put his arms around his father's shoulders and looked down at Holly woefully. 'Will you come and tuck me in?' he asked with a pleading tone in his voice.

'Of course I will.' Holly was on her feet immediately.

'That's very good of you, Holly,' Quinlan said with a shake of his head. 'I'm sorry about this. I hope your dinner won't be ruined.'

'I'm sure it will,' Fiona said with a frown. 'I don't think you should pander to the child——'

'We won't be long, Fiona.' Quin cut across her in a firm but polite voice. 'Don't let this spoil your meals. Please carry on.'

Fiona's eyes glittered with suppressed annoyance at this, and the look she sent Holly as she followed Quin from the room was anything but pleasant.

Quinlan led the way upstairs and Holly opened the door to Jamie's bedroom for him and then watched as he tenderly put him back into his bed. The room was the type that any child would just adore to have. It reminded Holly of the nurseries of bygone days. A large wooden rocking-horse stood at one side of the window. A toy fort with hand-painted soldiers stood at the other side. The shelves were neatly stacked with toys and books. A nightlight shaped like a carousel with colourful horses and the colourful lights of a carnival burnt brightly beside the bed.

'He is very hot,' Quinlan said over his shoulder to Holly.

She came further into the room and sat down on the side of the bed to look at the little boy. 'Have you any Calpol, Quinlan?' she asked as she put a gentle hand on the boy's forehead again.

'Yes, downstairs.' Quinlan turned to go and get it.

'And a bowl of cool water and a cloth while you're there,' she said before he could disappear.

Holly smiled reassuringly at Jamie when his dad had left them. 'You'll feel better when your dad gives you some medicine.'

He nodded solemnly. 'I didn't mean to be naughty and come downstairs,' he said in a worried tone. 'But I really didn't feel very well.'

'You were right to come down,' Holly told him softly.

'Aunty Fiona thinks I'm very bold,' Jamie said in a husky whisper. 'I don't think Aunty Fiona likes me very much; she's always cross with me.'

'Of course she likes you,' Holly assured him quickly. 'I'm sure she loves you very much.'

'Maybe.' Jamie didn't sound convinced and his little face looked strained with the effort of trying not to cry.

'Now then, Jamie, you are being very silly,' Holly said, gathering him into her arms. 'We all love you very much.' She stroked the top of his silky dark hair, surprised by how fiercely protective she felt towards the child.

Quinlan came back in then. One dark eyebrow lifted thoughtfully as he took in the scene before him. 'Sorry I was a while.' He sat down on the other side of the bed and put the bottle of medicine and the bowl of water on the table beside him. 'Come on, Jamie, are you going to take some of this medicine for me?'

The child sat back from Holly and rubbed his eyes in a gesture of complete tiredness. 'I suppose so.' He obediently opened his mouth as Quinlan poured the medicine for him. Then Holly sponged his forehead and around his neck in an attempt to cool him down.

Quinlan watched her gentle movements and smiled at her as their eyes met. 'Not quite the romantic evening you had planned,' he said in a low tone. 'I'm sorry, Holly.'

She shook her head. 'I really don't mind.' She flicked a glance up at him and smiled. 'Anyway, this is the least I can do. After all, it's not so long ago that you sat at my bedside when I was feeling ill.'

She put the bowl and the sponge down on the table as Jamie's eyes started to shut. 'Poor little thing,' she said softly. 'He's so tired.'

Quin put his hand to the boy's head. 'He doesn't seem quite as hot now. Hopefully he'll be back to his normal self in the morning.'

Holly nodded. 'If he isn't, be sure to call the doctor out straight away.' She tucked the sheet firmly around him and then stood up.

She watched as Quinlan bent and kissed his son, a strange feeling in the pit of her stomach as she noticed how tenderly he stroked the dark hair back from the hot little face before straightening. How wonderful it would be to be loved by Quinlan, she found herself thinking; to be held in his arms with such tenderness.

'Ready?' Quinlan glanced over at her and she nodded, all of a sudden her voice deserting her.

Leaving the door slightly ajar, they moved down the long corridor towards the staircase.

'Thank you, Holly.' Quin stopped just at the end of the corridor and caught hold of her arm before she could round the corner to the stairs. 'I appreciated your help with Jamie.'

She shook her head. 'You don't need to thank me,' she said softly, aware all the time of his hand resting against the soft skin of her inner arm. 'Anyway, I haven't really done anything... especially compared with what you've done for me.'

He frowned and the blue eyes seemed to cloud suddenly with a darkness that she couldn't fathom. 'For heaven's sake, can't you just forget for a moment that I was the one who brought you out of that fire?' he rasped harshly.

'Well... I...' She shook her head helplessly. She had never seen Quinlan lose his temper, and for some reason he seemed perilously close to it at the moment. She couldn't understand it; he was usually so laid-back. Even when she had openly insulted him in the past, he had laughed at her. Now, when she was thanking him, he seemed angry... she didn't know what to say to him.

'I... I'm sorry, Quin. It's just that...' Her voice trailed off as his head seemed to bend closer and the grip on her arm tightened. One moment she seemed to be standing looking up at him, the next she was in his arms. Had she swayed into the warmth of his embrace? Had she lifted her lips in an open invitation to his lips? Afterwards she wasn't quite sure how it had happened; all she knew was that it felt like heaven when his mouth touched hers; it sent shivers racing in tiny shooting spirals right down her back.

'Holly?' He murmured her name in a tone that sounded almost bemused. Then his kiss deepened. His hands moved around her waist, holding her so tightly that she felt her breath might be squeezed out of her body, yet she had never felt so exhilarated, so alive.

'Quinlan, I—oh!' The startled voice brought Holly back to reality.

Quinlan released her and turned his head, as did Holly, to look directly at Fiona, who had walked around the corner and nearly into them.

'I'm very sorry,' the woman said crisply, her eyes sparkling with an overbright gleam. 'I didn't realise that I would be interrupting anything.'

'That's all right,' Quinlan said easily. He seemed to have regained his composure completely, but then maybe he had never really lost it, Holly thought with a feeling of absolute chagrin. Had she just thrown herself at him?

'I was just coming to see if Jamie was all right,' Fiona went on coolly.

Holly doubted somehow that Fiona had been checking up on Jamie; more likely checking up on Quinlan, to see why he was so long.

'He's gone back to sleep.' Quinlan smiled down at Holly. 'Come on, let's go and finish our dinner. Poor Ross will think we've all deserted him.'

Holly felt sure that she wouldn't be able to eat another mouthful. Her heart was hammering wildly against her chest. She felt such a fool. The more Quinlan spoke in that relaxed, light-hearted tone, the more she was convinced that he thought her amusing...a joke. How could she have invited that kiss? How could she have left herself so vulnerable to him?

Ross looked up as they all came back into the room. He took one look at Fiona's face and looked at Holly with a lifted eyebrow. 'How's Jamie?'

'Not so bad now.' Somehow Holly managed to find her voice as she took her seat next to him.

'I didn't realise that you have medical training, Holly,' Fiona said archly.

'I don't. I just——'

'Then I suggest we call a doctor first thing in the morning.' Fiona cut across Holly and spoke directly to Quinlan. 'You can never be too careful.'

Quinlan nodded. 'Yes, Fiona, I do intend to call Dr Burns out tomorrow if there is no improvement,' he said in a patient tone.

'Good.' Fiona smiled across at Holly. 'No offence, Holly dear. But I do have a duty to see that the child is all right. He is my nephew and my sister would expect me to watch over him.' Somehow the woman made it sound as if Holly was in some way incompetent and her attempts at helping were only making things worse.

Holly nodded. 'Yes, of course,' she murmured, and just left the matter there. Obviously Fiona's anger stemmed from seeing her in Quinlan's arms, and she could hardly blame the woman. She wasn't sure what Fiona's relationship with Quin was... but obviously they were romantically involved if Quin was thinking of marrying her. Guilt flooded through her and she just toyed with the food in front of her, hardly daring even to glance across at Quin.

It was a relief when coffee was served in the lounge. They settled themselves in the deep settees and Quinlan put on some soothing background music. 'Would anyone like a liqueur?' he asked as he moved towards the drinks cabinet.

Holly shook her head as his glance moved towards her. She could feel her skin growing hot as their eyes met and she quickly looked away again.

'Quinlan tells me that you used to be a legal secretary in Dublin,' Fiona remarked as she sat opposite her.

Surprised by the friendly tone of the question, Holly glanced across at the woman and smiled. 'Yes, I worked for Richard Collins.'

'Did you?' Fiona seemed to brighten considerably. 'I know Richard very well. He lives a few doors down from me at Merrion Square.'

'What about you, Fiona?' Ross asked her suddenly. 'Do you work?'

The woman smiled. 'I dabble a little with stocks and shares,' she said, crossing her long legs and lounging back elegantly against the cushions of the settee. 'And

I have a boutique which I have left in the capable hands of a manageress.'

'Fiona is a very astute businesswoman,' Quinlan put in with a grin.

'Thank you, darling.' She smiled up at him as he handed her a cognac. 'And of course I have had invaluable help from you over the years. You've looked after me just as you did dear Camilla.'

'I've given you a few pieces of financial advice now and then,' Quinlan said a trifle drily. 'I would hardly compare it with the way I looked after Camilla.'

'Well, no...' For a moment Fiona looked flustered. Then she smiled over at Ross and Holly. 'Quinlan is very modest; he has doubled my investments in the last five years. I don't know what I'd do without him.'

'I'm sure, knowing you, Fiona, you would manage very well,' Quinlan said as he sat down beside her.

'I believe the stud farm is doing very well?' Ross asked with interest, and the conversation changed towards horses.

'Rather a boring subject,' Fiona yawned after a while. 'I'm not fond of horses.'

Holly couldn't help thinking that if that was the case the woman was not going to fit in very well at Montgomery House. Horses were a big part of Quinlan's life.

At last Ross looked at his watch and declared regretfully that it was time they should leave. Holly had been ready to go for the last couple of hours but she hadn't dared to be the one to suggest it.

'Yes, I suppose we should be heading for bed.' Fiona looked over at Quinlan and smiled. The look on her face made Holly's heart thud viciously. She looked across at Holly and there was a gleam of satisfaction in her eyes as she noticed that her words had hit their mark. 'These early mornings are killing me,' she continued smoothly.

'That's the only thing about living on a farm; the hours are ungodly.'

Holly forced herself to respond lightly. 'I rather like the early mornings, especially in the summer.'

'Well, you're probably just a country girl at heart,' Fiona said briskly, somehow making her sound more like a country bumpkin.

'Would you like to be back in Dublin?' Quinlan asked Holly suddenly.

Holly shook her head firmly. 'I love being on the farm. It's my home; I belong there.'

For a moment there was a strange expression on Quinlan's face, then he shrugged. 'It's unfortunate that the place doesn't belong to you,' he said drily.

Holly frowned. What on earth did that mean? 'Well, it was left to Flynn, him being the only son. But it is still my home,' she said quickly.

'I feel most at home in Dublin,' Fiona put in idly.

Why was she contemplating marrying a farmer, then? Holly asked herself wryly. Maybe she wasn't; maybe Quinlan hadn't asked her yet? Maybe when he did she would refuse? That thought brightened her up considerably as they walked out towards the front door.

Quinlan held her jacket for her and she tried very hard not to let her arms come into contact with him as she slid into it.

'Thank you for a lovely evening.' She summoned up a polite smile as she turned to face him again.

'You're very welcome.' There was a gleam of amusement in the blue eyes for a moment that made Holly feel most uncomfortable. Was he laughing at her? That would just be the last straw.

Then, much to her mortification, he leaned across towards her and kissed her cheek. She could feel her face burn as he straightened and looked down at her again. 'I enjoyed it very much,' he said with a twist of his lips. That threw her senses into complete turmoil. Was he talking about the kiss or the evening in general?

'You must come again soon,' Fiona put in crisply. One glance at the woman's face, however, told Holly that she would be anything but welcome.

'Yes,' Quinlan put in with a smile. 'Come over tomorrow, Holly. See how Jamie is going on.'

The invitation was issued almost like an order. 'Well, I don't know...' Holly hesitated, lost for an answer. She didn't want to come over here again tomorrow. Yet the thought of Jamie made her hesitate.

'I'm sure Holly will be far too busy,' Fiona put in firmly. Holly was almost grateful for her interruption; it saved her from having to make a reply.

Ross held out a hand towards Quinlan. 'Well, thanks again,' he said and then turned towards Fiona. 'Goodnight, Fiona.' He leaned across and kissed the woman's cheek.

Ross slanted an amused look over at Holly as they walked together towards his car. But he said nothing until they were safely inside and pulling away down the drive. 'You're a definite hit with Fiona,' he said on a note of amused sarcasm as they turned to wave to the couple who were standing in the lighted doorway watching their departure. Holly noticed idly that Fiona was now holding on to Quinlan's arm in a very proprietorial manner.

'I don't know what you mean,' she said as she turned away from them.

'No?' He flicked an amused glance over at her, then said, more seriously. 'Well, I would watch her, Holly. I'm not joking now. I'd say Fiona Matthews is out for your blood.'

'Nonsense.' Holly laughed off the idea. But there was a part of her that knew what Ross meant. Fiona would not be a nice person to be on the wrong side of, and she had a feeling that she was very much on the wrong side.

The lights were still on at the farm as Ross drove her up to her front door. 'Flynn must still be up,' Holly remarked idly. 'Would you like to come in for a coffee, Ross?'

'No, thanks, I'd better go. I have another early start tomorrow.'

She nodded and reached for the handle. Ross surprised her by catching hold of her arm as she turned.

'Yes?' She looked back at him, her eyes puzzled.

'You forgot something,' he said, and then leaned across towards her.

His kiss was light and gentle against her lips. There was no great explosion of feeling inside her such as she had felt when Quinlan had kissed her earlier. She pulled back from him and smiled. 'Thank you for a lovely evening,' she said sincerely.

For a moment there was a look of sadness on his face, then he shrugged. 'How about going for a drink some time?'

She nodded. 'That would be nice. Perhaps Sinead would like to come as well?'

'Perhaps... I'll give you a ring, then.'

She nodded and reached for the handle again. She liked Ross very much but she wanted to make it clear to him that he was just a friend. It wouldn't have been fair to give him any other idea.

She watched him drive away and then turned to go into the lounge.

Flynn was sitting at the large desk beside the window, concentrating very hard on some papers in front of him. He glanced over at her briefly and smiled. 'Had a good evening?' he asked, turning his attention back to his work.

'Not bad.' She put down her bag and walked over towards him. 'What are you doing?' she asked idly.

'Accounts.' He didn't look up, but Holly sensed a sudden tense atmosphere.

'I thought our accounts were up to date?' She frowned.

'Not quite.' Still he didn't look up at her.

Holly frowned. Maybe it was her imagination and Flynn was just busy, but he did seem very on edge.

She shrugged. 'Well, it's nice to see you taking an interest in the farm again, Flynn,' she said truthfully. 'I've been quite worried about the way you've been so unhappy here lately.'

That statement was met with silence. Then slowly Flynn turned to look at her. 'I have something to tell you, Holly,' he said seriously, and raked a hand through his hair in a distracted manner.

All of a sudden Holly's heart was surrounded by a coldness that seemed to gnaw at her very soul. She knew that whatever he was going to say was not something she was going to want to hear.

'I'm selling the farm. Quinlan has offered me a very fair price and I've accepted.'

The stark words hung heavily in the silence that followed. Holly could only stare at him in bewilderment, her insides churning in a painful way.

'How could you, Flynn?' When her voice came it was raw, almost as raw as when her lungs had been filled with black smoke. 'This is our home.'

Flynn shook his head. 'No, Holly. I've never been happy here. I've never wanted to be a farmer. I stuck it out for Dad's sake...because it was what he wanted. But it's not what I want.'

'It would break his heart to know you were selling,' Holly said with a shake of her head. 'Especially to Quinlan Montgomery. You know how he felt about that family.'

'Dad is dead, Holly.' Flynn's voice was firm. 'And we have to get on with our lives. My life isn't here. As for selling to a Montgomery...' Flynn shrugged. 'He is the only one to have offered me a good price. There can be no sentiment in business.'

Holly felt like crying all of a sudden. It was her home that he was talking about so coldly. It was a place where she had always felt safe... where happy memories of her parents, of her childhood surrounded her warmly. That he could just sell it without even a thought for her was incomprehensible.

'Don't look like that, Hol.' Flynn stood up, a heavy frown marring his good looks. 'This isn't something I've done lightly.' He hesitated for a moment and then continued. 'I know you're angry, but please try to understand.'

'You didn't even discuss it with me,' she said dully.

'I'm sorry, Holly, I never meant to hurt you.' Flynn looked unbearably sad for a moment. 'It's just that I've had a lot of pressures on me, a lot of financial problems that I didn't want to worry you with.' He raked his hand through his hair in a distraught manner. 'I had to sell, Holly, but I did consider you. The first time that Quinlan made an offer for the place I refused. I told him straight that your feelings towards him were the reason I couldn't accept. That there was no way I could sell to him unless your feelings mellowed towards him.'

'And then, miraculously, they did,' Holly said coldly. Suddenly it all started to make sense. Why else had Quinlan invited her out to dinner and on picnics? He had been trying to charm her around so that Flynn would agree to the sale.

'Come on, Holly, it's not so bad...' Flynn's voice trailed off as she turned and left the room.

She raced up the stairs and into her bedroom. Then she stood at the window staring out into the blackness of the summer night. She was homeless—the thought wove in and out of her other thoughts.

Quinlan Montgomery was going to possess everything that she held most precious in life. Along with the awful sense of loss was an even greater one of betrayal. Quinlan had only invited her out to get around Flynn. How he must be laughing at her. Her heart felt suddenly as if it would break. What on earth was she going to do?

CHAPTER SEVEN

'SO WHAT are you going to do?' Sinead asked her as she sat down on Holly's bed and watched her pack.

Holly shrugged. 'Rent a flat in Dublin and try and get another job.'

'Easier said than done in the present economic climate,' Sinead murmured. 'Any chance of you getting your old job back at the solicitors?'

'I rang them last week.' Holly continued to fold her clothes into one of the big suitcases on the floor as she spoke. 'They said they were very sorry but they've already replaced me.'

'Hardly surprising, I suppose.' Sinead pushed a hand through her dark silky hair in a worried gesture. 'I must say I think it's dreadful of Flynn to rush you out like this. You were so good giving up your job and coming to help him when he needed it most. He could at least have delayed the sale on this place until you got yourself sorted out.'

'Well, Quinlan offered him a good price for the place on condition that the sale went through quickly,' Holly said in a matter-of-fact voice, then sighed. 'I suppose I can't blame Flynn. Let's face it, Sinead, there aren't many buyers around with that kind of money at the moment, and Flynn did have a lot of debts that he was just too scared to tell me about.'

'I suppose so.' There was a silence for a moment. 'Is Flynn still talking about going to Australia?'

Holly nodded. 'Short-term at first. He's going out for a few months to see how he likes it. Then he's going to apply to become a permanent resident.' It was strange how she could talk about it so calmly. The thought of Flynn going all those thousands of miles away was like a knife turning inside her.

The silence stretched and Holly glanced across at her friend. She was surprised to see that Sinead was looking very upset.

'Sinead, what's wrong?' She moved to sit beside her on the bed, reaching for her hand in a gesture of concern.

'Nothing.' Sinead sniffed and tried very hard to smile, but it was a brave attempt that went sadly wrong. She shook her head. 'It's just... the thought of Flynn going away,' she admitted in a low tone.

'You're upset at Flynn leaving?' Holly was completely stunned by this and just stared at her friend for a moment in complete amazement.

Sinead gave a shaky laugh. 'Don't look at me like that, Holly. I know it's totally ludicrous. It surprised me as well. I didn't think I was at all bothered about Flynn until he said he was going.' She looked up at her friend. 'Tell me I'm completely crazy,' she said in a broken whisper. 'I know I am.'

'You're completely crazy,' Holly complied with a smile and then put her arm around her friend. 'If that's how you feel then tell him, Sinead,' she urged softly. 'I know Flynn has always liked you very much. Perhaps you'll end up going to Australia with him.'

Sinead shook her head. 'I don't want to go to Australia. Ireland is my home, Holly.'

'Well, tell him anyway. Maybe he'll change his mind about going,' Holly said with a glimmer of hope in her voice now.

'No.' Sinead shook her head. 'It wouldn't be fair. Flynn wants to go to Australia; it's his dream. I can't stand in his way.'

Holly frowned. 'But maybe if he had you in his life he would be content to stay.'

'No, Holly. I couldn't take that risk. "Maybe" is a big word. I would hate him just to stay for my sake; if it didn't work out he would always blame me for ruining his chances of emigrating.' Sinead looked up at Holly with bright, shimmering eyes. 'I can't tell him, Holly. And you must promise me that you won't say anything.'

Holly hesitated.

'Please.' Sinead's voice was desperately pleading.

Holly shrugged. 'All right, I promise. But I still think you should tell him.'

The girl shook her head and then made a determined effort to brighten up. 'I'm supposed to be cheering you up,' she said with a smile. 'And somehow it's ended the other way around.'

'Oh, I'm not so bad,' Holly said with a note of determination in her voice. 'I'm made of quite tough stuff, you know.'

'Yes, I've noticed,' Sinead said with a laugh. 'You know, you're welcome to come and stay with me for a while. I've only got one bedroom in my flat, as you know, but it would be no trouble to make some room for you.'

Holly shook her head. 'Thanks, Sinead, but I've got to sort myself out sooner or later. Better it's sooner.' She nodded towards a paper sitting on the bedside table. 'I've already got a few flats ringed in there that I'm going to take a look at.'

'Well, the offer is always open,' Sinead said briskly. 'And then there's Ross. He's all alone in that big house of his. I'm sure he would be very pleased to offer you a room.'

'I don't think that would be a good idea,' Holly said as she got up from the bed. 'I need to find work, Sinead, and I'm sorry to say that there won't be much of that going around here. I have no other choice than to go back to the city.'

There was a noise of a car pulling up outside and Sinead crossed to the window to look out. 'It's Quin,' she said, turning towards Holly.

Holly made a face. She had avoided seeing Quinlan since that dinner party last week. Although he had been around to the house on two occasions she had made sure she was out when he came.

The doorbell rang and Holly hesitated.

'Well, aren't you going to let him in?' Sinead asked with interest.

'He'll only have come to speak to Flynn,' said Holly drily. 'Do me a favour, Sinead. Go down and tell him Flynn isn't here. He should be back around four,' she said, glancing at her watch.

'What if he wants to speak to you?' Sinead asked with a grin.

'He won't.' Holly started to carry on with her packing. 'But if he does,' she added quickly as the girl moved towards the door, 'tell him I'm not here either.'

'That's not very nice, Holly,' Sinead said reprovingly.

'Well, I'm not in a very nice mood where that man is concerned,' Holly said firmly.

She continued to throw things into the suitcase, half listening as Sinead went downstairs and opened the door.

She heard the low murmur of voices, but couldn't make out what either was saying. She resisted the temptation to tiptoe to the door and listen. She didn't care what Quinlan had to say. If she never saw him again it would be a day too soon. She heard the front door close again and the crunch of footsteps across the gravel drive outside and heaved a sigh of relief.

'Thanks, Sinead,' she said over her shoulder as the bedroom door opened. 'I don't want to see Quinlan Montgomery ever again. He's a snake.'

'Don't you know that St Patrick drove all the snakes out of Ireland a long, long time ago?' a male voice answered with a gleam of amusement.

Holly whirled around to see Quin standing in her bedroom as large as life itself. He looked fabulous too. He was wearing a pair of fawn chinos and a cream silk shirt. His dark hair gleamed black as coal in the afternoon sunlight that streamed through the window.

'What are you doing in here?' she demanded sharply, her face going a deep crimson as anger washed through her.

'I've come to speak to you,' he answered easily.

'Sinead shouldn't have let you in. I told her that I didn't want to speak to you.' Holly turned and continued throwing things into her case with brisk, angry movements.

Unperturbed, Quinlan moved to sit on her bed and watched her with a kind of lazy amusement.

'I really don't want you in here,' Holly told him furiously as she finished putting the last of her clothes from the wardrobe into the case. Added to her anger was the embarrassing recollection of how she had flung herself at him the other night. The memory of that kiss made her heart start to thud painfully in her chest.

'You won't be able to close that,' Quinlan observed as she struggled to shut the lid. 'Would you like a hand?'

'No, I wouldn't. I don't want anything from you,' she snapped.

'Please yourself.' He picked up the newspaper that was sitting next to the bed. 'Looking for a flat, I see.'

She made no reply, just glanced up at him with eyes that spoke volumes, before lifting the lid of her suitcase and taking a few of the excess items out to transfer them to another bag.

'I don't think you'll be happy with any of the ones you've ringed,' Quinlan continued. 'They're not in the best of areas.'

'I haven't the best of finances,' she said drily. 'So they'll have to do until I get a job.'

'I thought you didn't want to go back to Dublin,' he said.

'Are you trying to be funny?' She glared at him, her eyes as bright as a cat's in the beam of strong lights.

'No. I was just asking you a question,' he said levelly. His eyes moved over the glossy sheen of her auburn hair as he spoke and then down over her slender figure in the close-fitting white cotton shirt and faded Levi jeans.

'I'm going back to town because I haven't any other choice,' she told him briskly. 'I would have thought that was obvious.'

'There is always a choice,' he said quietly.

Holly raised her eyebrows in disdain. Only someone with Quinlan's wealth could think like that, she thought drily. She didn't bother to answer him. She had finally got the first suitcase closed and was now working on the second.

'Why are you so angry with me, Holly?' he asked, putting the newspaper down and standing up.

She would have preferred him to remain sitting. When he was standing above her like that she felt at a distinct disadvantage. 'You've been avoiding me for over a week now.'

'I think the reason must be pretty obvious, even to you,' she grated sarcastically.

'I've offered your brother a fair price for the farm,' he said briskly. 'He wants very much to sell.'

'I don't think Flynn knows what he wants at the moment,' Holly murmured.

'So you're of the opinion that I'm taking advantage of a man in a weak emotional state,' he grated. 'Is that what you think?'

'I think you could have mentioned to me that you were interested in the property. You never said one word to me about it.' She sat back on her heels and looked up at him. 'I think you behaved in a devious and underhand manner.'

'Do you, now?' For a moment he sounded amused. 'And when should I have discussed this business with you? When you were sick in bed after the fire? On the beach when our friendship had only just found a tenuous beginning? Over dinner with Fiona and Ross? When would you have considered the time right?' he enquired mockingly. 'Because I can assure you that, whenever I chose to mention it, there would have been no rational discussion. You would have been just as angry as you are right now.'

'So you have me taped for just an irrational female? Is that it, Quinlan?' She got slowly to her feet and lifted her head with a dignified tilt to meet his eyes. 'Well, let me tell you, I'm as capable of behaving in a cool, unemotional way as any man. As for my not being well...I had smoke in my lungs, not on my brain.'

His lips twisted with dry humour. 'Then come out to lunch with me and we'll talk.'

The invitation completely threw her. It was the last thing she'd expected. 'I don't want to have lunch with you.' She backed away a step. 'We have nothing to talk about.'

'Now who's being irrational?' He smiled. 'I have a business proposition for you.'

She frowned. 'What about?'

'Come to lunch and find out.'

She hesitated. Her curiosity was aroused, but she didn't really want to go out to lunch with him.

He laughed. 'So much for the talk about being able to discuss things in a cool, unemotional way.'

'For heaven's sake, Quinlan, I haven't time to play games——'

'Neither have I. Will you come to lunch or won't you? The choice is yours.' He cut across her with an infuriating note in his voice.

She should have refused the offer, should have told him to go to hell...but somehow she couldn't; somehow she was afraid that if she did he would walk out of her life and she would always wonder what he'd been going to say.

He smiled as he noted the change in her expression. 'I'll wait for you downstairs,' he said, and turned to leave her.

Holly glared at his back. He was so arrogant, so sure of himself. She wished heatedly that she had the strength of mind to tell him not to bother waiting. Instead she turned and started rummaging through her clothes for a suitable outfit to go for lunch in.

She chose a pale buttercup skirt that stopped just above the knee, and a jacket that was plain yet looked elegant. As she flicked a brush through her long hair and studied her reflection critically in the full-length mirror she wondered what on earth she was doing. Why was she taking such care over her appearance? She didn't care what Quinlan thought of her. Irritated with herself, she picked up her bag and hurried downstairs.

He was in the lounge studying the picture of Lucinda Fitzgerald. He turned with a smile as she came into the room. 'I always admire that painting.'

'Well, I suppose it belongs to you now,' Holly said drily. She tried very hard to sound as if she didn't care; she didn't want to give him the satisfaction of knowing how much it hurt her to think of her family's estate in his possession.

'Not yet,' he said casually.

Anger bubbled inside her. 'You do realise that my horse Becky is not included in the sale, I hope?' she asked in a brittle tone. 'She belongs to me.'

'Yes, I do know that,' he replied levelly, then smiled. 'Are you ready?' His eyes moved over her with a gleam of male appreciation that instantly sent a wave of heat sweeping through her.

'Yes.' She turned away and walked ahead of him towards the front door. It opened just as she reached it and she practically collided with her brother.

'Hello.' Flynn's glance moved with surprise to Quinlan. 'Are you looking for me?'

'No.' Quinlan slipped his hand on Holly's waist. 'I just called to see if Holly would come out to lunch.'

'I see.' Flynn grinned at his sister. 'Well, have a good time.'

Holly would have had some cutting remark to make about that, but Quinlan propelled her forward and out of the door before she could speak.

She glared at him as they walked towards his car. 'I was just about to say something back there,' she told him frostily.

'I know.' He opened the door of the red Lotus sports car for her. 'But I figured there's no point upsetting Flynn. It's made his day seeing us going out like civilised friends.' The door slammed closed on her as she settled herself into the deep seat.

'And of course you want to keep him happy until the sale is completed,' she said scathingly as he got into the driving seat.

'Of course,' he agreed easily as he started the powerful engine.

Her hands tightened into small fists as they rested on her lap. 'Is that the reason you've invited me out?' she asked briskly.

'No.' He flicked an amused glance at her.

'But it is the reason why you've suddenly become so friendly recently?' She asked the question briskly, before she lost her courage.

'Is that what you think?' One eyebrow lifted in surprise.

'What else is there to think?' she said tautly.

'Well, you're wrong, Holly.' He changed the car up into fifth gear and it cruised easily down the lanes that led towards the Glen of the Downs.

Holly didn't think she was wrong at all and she noticed that Quinlan made no attempt to persuade her otherwise. The subject was dropped and Holly tried to clear her mind of the hurt she felt inside. She didn't care about his motives. Very soon she would be back in Dublin and Quinlan would just be a distant memory.

She stared out at the passing scenery. The Glen of the Downs was a very picturesque spot. At each side of the road the trees came down steep mountains, fringing the road in deep leafy green.

They travelled in silence until Quinlan turned the car through gates and up a winding drive towards a large, impressive hotel that nestled high above the road, with sweeping views out across the countryside.

'I haven't been here for ages,' Holly remarked idly. 'It brings back memories.'

'Really?' Quin parked the car and turned to look at her. 'Who were you here with?'

'My parents, Flynn, Ross and Sinead,' she said lightly. 'It was my birthday.'

There was silence for a moment. 'I'm sorry, Holly. Would you rather go somewhere else?'

'No.' She frowned. 'It's all right, Quinlan. If I were to try and avoid all the places that bring back memories of my parents, there wouldn't be a lot of places left to go around here.'

'I suppose not.' He smiled ruefully.

'Anyway, they're happy memories.' She glanced away from him and up at the hotel. 'I was lucky; I had a lovely childhood, very good parents.'

'Yes, you were.' His voice was gentle.

She glanced around at him. What was his childhood like? she found herself thinking. She knew his mother had died when he was young. Holly didn't remember her at all. But she remembered his father. She had always thought him very austere, a little bit frightening. Had Quinlan's childhood been lonely? She frowned, not liking the thought.

'Come on, then.' He opened the door and climbed out into the bright, sunny afternoon, his manner once more brisk and authoritative. It was ridiculous to think of Quinlan in any way vulnerable or lonely, she chided herself as she got out to join him. He had probably been born arrogant and businesslike. The thought conjured up an image of Quin as a baby, clutching a briefcase and telling his father that the farm wasn't cost-effective. She smiled to herself at the silly thought.

'What's so funny?' He glanced sideways at her.

'Nothing.' She shook her head quickly. The sun gleamed on the silky strands of her hair, highlighting its fiery tones, and for a moment his attention seemed distracted as his eyes moved over her. She frowned as she noticed how he was looking at her, and her heart seemed to do a funny kind of twist inside her.

Quinlan smiled at her and opened the door to let her precede him into the hotel. It was relatively quiet inside and they were shown to a table almost immediately.

'Is this all right?' Quinlan checked with her before they took their seats at one of the best tables with views out over the countryside.

'Fine.' She accepted the menu the waiter handed her as she settled herself in the seat facing Quin.

'If you would prefer to sit somewhere else——' Quinlan started to say as the waiter left them.

'Quin, I'm fine,' she cut across him firmly, and glared down at the menu in front of her. Her heart was still racing from that strange way he had looked at her outside. It was most disconcerting how he could throw her into turmoil with just a look. And she didn't care for his phoney concern over where she sat. As if he really cared if she was upset over the seating arrangements! The idea was ludicrous when he knew she was here under sufferance anyway.

Why had he invited her to lunch? she wondered anxiously. Just what kind of game was he playing now? Deep inside her there was a flutter of nerves. She wished she hadn't come; it was a mistake, she just knew it was.

'So have you decided?' His deep voice interrupted her thoughts and she realised that she had been frowning at the menu for ages without really reading it.

'I'll have the prawns followed by chicken *à la crème*,' she said, shutting the menu card decisively.

Quinlan held up his hand to indicate to the waiter that they were ready to order.

'Would you like some wine with your food?' Quinlan asked her after he had placed the food order. 'Or just spring water?'

About to order her usual sparkling water, she changed her mind. Maybe one glass of wine would help relax her.

Quinlan's eyebrows lifted as she accepted the offer of wine.

'So you do drink the occasional alcoholic beverage,' he said with a smile as the waiter left them.

'Sometimes.' She shrugged.

He smiled at her. 'You are certainly not predictable, Miss Fitzgerald.'

'Neither are you, Mr Montgomery.' She matched his tone and then forced herself to meet those sparkling blue eyes across the table in a businesslike way. 'So, are you going to tell me what all this is about? I hardly think you've invited me to lunch to find out my taste in fine foods.'

'You'd be surprised what I'm interested in,' he murmured with a smile.

She was glad that the waiter arrived at that moment with their drinks. Her heart had started to beat in a most uncomfortable way again. She wished Quin wouldn't tease her like that; it made it almost impossible to remain coolly indifferent to him.

'So is Flynn still talking about going to Australia?' he changed the subject, much to her relief. Although she noticed that he hadn't made any attempt to answer her question.

'Yes, he is.' She reached for her glass.

'And how do you feel about that?'

She glared across at him. 'On top of the world,' she grated sarcastically. 'How do you think I feel?'

He shrugged. 'Would you like me to try and talk to him about it?'

'If I can't talk him out of it, I don't think you'll have much chance.'

He smiled. 'I think you're underestimating my persuasive powers,' he said silkily.

Maybe she was, she acknowledged silently. But she certainly wasn't underestimating the power of the attraction she felt towards him. Every time she caught the full force of his smile it seemed to knock her sideways. Her hands tightened around the slender stem of her wine glass. She wasn't in love with him, she told herself firmly, just as she had told herself every day since that dinner party. It was just a physical attraction, nothing more.

'I don't know why you would bother to try and persuade Flynn to stay in Ireland anyway,' she said crisply, refusing to soften towards that magnetic charm. 'I shouldn't think you care what he does, just as long as you have his farm.'

The blue eyes narrowed. 'You don't have me pegged as a very nice person, do you, Holly?'

The question threw her, and she shrugged. 'I'm not sure what kind of a person you are,' she answered truthfully. 'I don't really know you.'

The conversation was interrupted by the arrival of their first course. When the waiter had left them, Holly took the opportunity to change the subject from the personal level it had descended to. 'How's Jamie?' she asked.

'He's fine. He had a temperature for a few days but it didn't lead to anything.'

Holly nodded. She already knew that the child was on the way to recovery; she had asked Flynn to enquire every time he was meeting with Quin.

'He was disappointed that you didn't come over to see him,' Quinlan continued drolly. 'He thinks a great deal of you.'

Holly immediately felt guilty. She had wanted to go and visit him but she had dreaded bumping into Quinlan. 'I think a lot of him as well,' she said truthfully.

'Yes, it constantly surprises me how well you get on with him.'

'Why shouldn't I?' She frowned over at him. 'He is a sweet and very lovable child.'

'He is also a Montgomery,' Quinlan said drily.

Holly smiled for a moment. 'I don't hold it against him.'

'Yet you hold it against me,' he stated with a lift of one dark eyebrow. About to tell him that he wasn't sweet and lovable, she suddenly changed her mind about the wisdom of that and merely shrugged.

'You didn't come over because you were afraid of bumping into me, isn't that right?'

'I wasn't afraid,' she told him with a frown, then added drily, 'but you haven't been on my list of most likeable men these last few days.'

'I don't think I've ever made that list, have I?' he asked softly.

There was something about his tone that made Holly feel warm inside. It was a strange sensation, as if she was melting inside. Then, when she met those eyes, she could almost feel her toes curling. 'No.' She tried to wipe out the feeling very firmly with the negative word and a shake of her head. 'And let's face it, Quin, your behaviour lately has just reinforced all my earlier impressions of you.'

He lifted his glass to his lips, taking his time about answering her, his manner relaxed, unperturbed. 'By my behaviour, I suppose you're referring to my buying Fitzgerald Farm?' he asked drily.

'You know damn well that I am. You deliberately set out to befriend me, knowing that it would make for easier negotiation with my brother.' Her eyes blazed across at him, alive with anger and a fair dash of hurt as well.

'Come on, Holly.' There was a note of impatience in his tone for a moment. 'I've already told you that my friendship with you has nothing to do with the sale of the farm. Next you'll be accusing me of saving you from that fire in the stables just so I could get into Flynn's good books.'

She frowned. She wished he hadn't mentioned that episode. The last thing she wanted was to feel indebted to him. 'Maybe you did,' she said glibly, then promptly regretted the words as she saw the ominous dark look of anger starting to cloud his face. 'I'm sorry, Quin,' she said hurriedly. 'I don't really think that. I really am very grateful for what you did that night.'

The look of anger didn't disappear at the apology. He made no reply for a moment, just sat studying her with a kind of brooding dark stare.

Holly could feel her heart thudding nervously at that look on his face.

'Just how grateful are you?' he asked suddenly, making her edge back on her chair apprehensively.

'I beg your pardon?' Apart from a tiny tremor, her voice was cool and angry. Just what was he implying? Her befuddled mind wrestled with his question, half afraid, half furious.

'I asked you how grateful you feel towards me,' he repeated the question crisply. 'Because I have a proposition for you.'

The waiter chose that moment to arrive and clear the table and present them with their main course. Holly watched him serve it with a feeling of intense dread. What the hell was Quin going to ask her? She swallowed on the dry feeling in her throat and tried to think rationally. The trouble was that all sorts of very unsavoury ideas were starting to form in her mind, so much so that when the waiter left them she found that her hands were shaking so much she couldn't possibly pick up her cutlery. Instead she clenched them tightly in her lap and waited breathlessly for Quin to continue.

He on the other hand was very relaxed. He lifted his fork and tried a little of the food in front of him before glancing across at her. 'What's the matter, have you lost your appetite?' he asked.

Holly saw the gleam of amusement returning to his blue eyes and frowned. He was toying with her, deliberately winding her up. With an effort of will she forced herself to pick up her knife and fork. 'No. I was waiting for you to continue,' she managed to say lightly. 'What's your proposition?'

Instead of answering her immediately, he leaned across and refilled her glass with some more wine. 'What are your plans now that you'll be leaving the farm?'

Holly glared at him, infuriated by the change of subject. 'You know that already. I'm looking for another office job in Dublin. What has that to do with what we were discussing?'

'Quite a lot, actually,' he replied calmly. 'Because I want you to come and work for me.'

'Work for you!' Holly's voice rose a couple of decibels and some people at another table glanced across at them curiously. 'You must be crazy. You're the last person I would want to work for,' she continued heatedly, regardless of anyone who might overhear.

Quin looked amused. 'Why not? I think your working for me is the perfect solution to all our problems.'

'I don't think it answers any of *my* problems,' Holly said drily. 'And I wasn't aware that you had any.'

'Oh, but I do,' Quin said with a wry curve of his lips. 'And I think you could solve them all.' He reached for his wine glass. 'I need someone to look after Jamie; I also need someone to do some office work, someone who is familiar with the workings of a farm. You would be ideal.' He took a sip of his wine and placed the glass down before continuing smoothly. 'Jamie likes you, and I believe you're a very competent secretary. The ideal Girl Friday.'

Holly shook her head; she couldn't believe what she was hearing.

'I think you would be a lot happier living at Montgomery House than in a flat in Dublin. Plus you can stable Becky there and ride her whenever you want.'

'Live at your house?' Holly repeated the words numbly, then shook her head. 'No, Quin.'

One dark eyebrow lifted. 'You haven't even thought about it.'

'I don't need to think about it,' she said staunchly. The thought of living under the same roof as Quinlan made her nerves tangle into a million knots. 'Anyway, you have Fiona to look after Jamie.'

The look Quinlan gave her as she said those words spoke volumes. 'Fiona has a lot of good qualities but childminding isn't one of them,' he said drily. 'If she had her way I would be sending Jamie to a boarding-school next year.'

'But you would never seriously think of that as a possibility,' Holly said in horrified tones.

Quinlan hesitated and there was a speculative gleam in his blue eyes for a moment. 'You don't like the idea?' he asked softly.

'You know I don't.' Holly leaned across the table, her eyes bright with emotion. 'He's a baby, Quin; you can't send him away.'

'I might have no other choice,' Quinlan said with a shrug. 'Fiona certainly can't look after him full-time, and getting a full time childminder whom I can trust is no easy task.'

Holly shook her head, her eyes glimmering with anger. It seemed so heartless to just pack the child away to boarding-school. She couldn't bear the thought.

'So what do you say?' he asked her softly. 'Will you help me out and give the job a try?'

Holly stared across at him, torn between the tenderness in her heart for the little boy and the apprehension at living under the same roof as Quinlan Montgomery.

CHAPTER EIGHT

'YOU are to sleep in here.' Fiona opened the door to a very luxurious bedroom and led the way in. 'You have your own bathroom through there.' She opened up the door to the side and then turned to face Holly as she put her small holdall down beside the bed. 'Jamie's room is next door and Quin and I are further down the hall.'

Holly kept a carefully bland expression at this piece of information. 'Fine,' she said lightly. Yet there was a strange twist in her heart. Fiona was sleeping with Quin. She shouldn't have been surprised; it was really quite obvious that Fiona was romantically involved with him. Yet deep in her heart she was still upset at the blatancy of the words. Then she was annoyed with herself because she was upset.

'We have dinner at six. Usually we'll want you to bath Jamie after dinner and settle him down. That won't be necessary tonight,' Fiona continued in cool, crisp tones.

Holly fought down a feeling of resentment at the woman's tone. She had come here to work, so she shouldn't mind Fiona dishing out a few instructions. Yet she resented the woman's attitude. It was as if this were Fiona's house and Holly were here to work for her, not Quin.

'I'll show you Quin's office after you've unpacked,' the woman continued.

'No need, Fiona,' Quin's voice interrupted them from the door. 'I'll show Holly around the office later.' He came into the room and put her heavy cases down next to the wardrobe. 'I hope you'll be comfortable in here, Holly,' he said, turning to look at her.

'I'm sure I will,' Holly answered politely.

'Right, then, we'll leave you to settle in.' He held the door for Fiona to precede him from the room. 'Do you need any help to unpack? I can send Mary up.' He lingered in the doorway and for a moment his eyes moved over her slender figure.

'No, I can manage, thank you.' She heaved a sigh of relief as he nodded then turned and shut the door behind him.

What was she doing here? she wondered with a pang of anguish as she sat down on the bed. It was exactly a week since Quin had taken her out to lunch and offered her this job. She should never have accepted it, she knew that with certainty. It was only the fact that Quin had appealed to the soft side of her nature, the side that cried out against a small child being sent away from his home at such a tender age, that had changed her mind. She raked a tired hand through her hair and stood up to sort out her suitcases. If things didn't work out, she would leave at the end of the month. She had told Quinlan that she was only giving the job a month's trial. With that reassuring thought she turned to the task of unpacking.

Once everything was hanging in the wardrobe Holly glanced at her watch. She just had time to shower before dinner. She selected a casual pair of beige trousers and a plain cream blouse and then went through to the bathroom.

The rooms were certainly beautiful, she thought idly as she undressed. Both were decorated in a country style, peach and cream colours co-ordinating from the bedroom through to the bathroom. Pine furniture and dried flower arrangements added to the cosy, warm feeling of the décor.

After her shower she dried her hair hurriedly and dressed. She studied her reflection in the full-length mirror of the bedroom. She looked poised and cool, her hair sitting perfectly in thick glossy waves around her shoulders. Her skin had a delicate tinge of colour from the shower, her eyes were wide and clear. There was no trace of the turmoil inside her. With a sigh she turned away from the mirror and glanced out of the window.

Below her the lawns were perfectly manicured, as if someone had rolled down a piece of bright emerald carpet. The trees that bordered the lawn were just starting to show the tinge of colour which signified that autumn was not far away, the ruby-red berries on the rowan trees contrasting vividly against the blue of the sky. Fitzgerald Farm had never had such well tended gardens. The view from her old bedroom window had looked out on to the cobbled front yard. Her old bedroom had had none of the luxury of this one. Yet, strangely, she felt a terrible pang of homesickness.

So much had changed this year. What would her parents think about Flynn selling the farm to Quinlan Montgomery? She tried to imagine their reaction, her father's face. What would they say if they knew she was living in the Montgomery House? That she was in love with Quinlan Montgomery?

She turned away from the view and swallowed hard. No... not in love, just infatuated, she corrected herself with a haste borne of sheer anguish.

There was a tap at the door and Quinlan's voice made her jump.

'Holly, can I come in?'

'Yes.' She forced herself to cross towards the door and face him. She was being utterly ridiculous imagining herself in love with him. She needed to get a grip on her wayward emotions, she told herself furiously. Yet her heart thudded wildly when she opened the door and saw him standing there.

'You look lovely.' He smiled at her. She noticed that when he smiled his eyes lit up warmly.

'Thanks.' Her voice was brisk as she desperately strove to pull herself together. 'Did you want something?'

One dark eyebrow lifted. 'If you have a few moments I'd like to show you around the office before dinner, familiarise you with the filing system, that kind of thing.'

'Fine.' She closed the door behind her. 'Lead on.'

For a moment there was a glimmer of amusement on his handsome features. 'I see you've snapped into office mode already.'

'I beg your pardon?' She looked up at him, trying very hard not to notice how handsome he was.

'The efficient, brisk manner,' he explained drily.

She shrugged. 'I'm an employee now. I would have thought you would want me to be brisk and efficient.'

'As long as you don't carry it too far.' His lips twisted into a wry smile. 'We're still friends.'

About to tell him that they had never really been friends, she changed her mind abruptly and instead changed the subject. 'Are you going to show me the office or not?'

He shrugged and turned to lead the way.

There was a surprising amount of paperwork waiting to be sorted out in the office. Most of the correspondence was concerned with the stud farm, but there were other businesses that Holly didn't know anything about.

'I didn't realise you owned so much around here,' she remarked idly as he showed her each separate file.

'Don't worry. There isn't much for you to do. When Jamie starts back to school next week I'd like you to do a few hours each morning in here. That's about it,' he said matter-of-factly.

'I wasn't complaining,' she said with a frown. 'You're paying me a very good salary. I expect to be kept busy.'

'All I want is for you to take Jamie to and from school, spend some time with him and a couple of hours in here. The rest of the time is your own.' He started to lock all the files again then turned to look at her. 'I want you to be happy here, Holly,' he said softly.

Holly swallowed hard. She hated it when Quin spoke to her like that. It gave her that warm kind of melting feeling inside, made her heart start to behave in a very erratic way.

'Thank you.' She forced herself to smile at him in a polite way.

He smiled. 'And I think you are going to make a very efficient secretary-cum-childminder.'

'Well, we'll see,' Holly answered cautiously. 'As I said before, this is just a trial, Quin. If either of us is not satisfied with the way things work out, we can call it quits at the end of next month.'

'Oh, I think things will work out, Holly.' There was that note in his voice again. The blue eyes were incredibly warm as they travelled over her face.

She looked away from him, feeling embarrassed as her body flew so easily into chaos. She wasn't so sure that things were going to work out at all.

There was a tap on the door and Fiona put her head around. 'Dinner is ready,' she said.

'OK.' Quin smiled at Holly. 'You go ahead; I'll just finish putting things away in here.'

Holly nodded and went to walk with Fiona towards the dining-room.

She had changed, Holly noticed idly. This afternoon she had been wearing a classic beige dress; now she was wearing a black mini-skirt and a figure-hugging gold and black top that showed the curves of her figure in a very sexy way. She looked like a blonde Barbie doll, her eyes heavily made-up with blue mascara and her lips painted a deep red.

'I thought that Quin and I could go out this evening,' she said with a smile at Holly as they took their seats at the dining-room table. 'Now that we have you to look after Jamie, things should be better.'

'Where is he?' Holly asked. She didn't like the way the woman spoke about the child, as if he were some kind of an inconvenience.

'I had to send him to bed early this afternoon. He was extremely naughty.' Fiona flicked her napkin out in an angry movement. 'The child is impossible—I don't envy you the job of looking after him.'

'Why? What did he do?' Holly frowned. Jamie didn't really strike her as an impossibly naughty child.

'Gave me a lot of cheek.' Fiona glared over at her. 'I've told him that if he doesn't buck up and behave himself we will be sending him off to boarding-school. That seemed to quieten him down for a while.'

Holly bit down on an angry retort. It seemed to her that Jamie wasn't the one at fault. Fiona obviously just had no idea how to handle the child. 'I don't think you really get good results with children by threatening them like that,' she said quietly.

'Pardon me, Holly, but I don't really think you're qualified to say.' Fiona glanced across at her in a very cool manner. 'I'm frankly very surprised that Quinlan has gone ahead and hired someone such as yourself, someone with absolutely no qualifications as a childminder.'

Holly shrugged. 'I was surprised as well,' she said evenly. 'I can only give it my best shot, and I am very fond of Jamie.'

'Well, we shall just have to wait and see how things go.' The woman's tone left Holly in no doubt that it would be Holly who would go.

'Yes.' Holly just agreed with her. Clearly Fiona was not pleased at her being here. She could only do her best and hope that she wouldn't see too much of the woman.

Quinlan joined them at that point, much to Holly's relief. She wondered what he thought about Fiona's attitude towards his child. Was he still contemplating marrying her? Surely he would give some consideration to the fact that Fiona was just not cut out to be a surrogate mother?

'Fiona was just telling me that she had to send Jamie to bed.' Holly couldn't resist probing a little.

Quinlan nodded. 'He was just overtired—poor kid hasn't been sleeping too well since that bout of flu last week.' Quin smiled across at her. 'Plus he was very excited when I told him you were coming to live with us.'

The way Quin said the words 'coming to live with us' made Holly's stomach tie itself in knots. He made it sound so personal, and for one silly moment she couldn't help wishing that it were that intimate, that she were here to live with Quinlan. Immediately she thrust that thought away. It was going to be hard enough staying under the same roof as Quinlan without thinking things like that.

She glanced away from him, then caught the glare of Fiona's eyes across the table. They were glittering with an intensity that Holly found strangely chilling.

Somehow Holly managed to do justice to the beautiful dinner that Mary placed before them, but it was a relief when the dinner came to an end. She found it a strain making polite conversation with Fiona and even more so with Quinlan.

As soon as Quin suggested that they take coffee in the lounge Holly excused herself. 'If you don't mind, Quin, I won't have a coffee. I thought I'd just walk around the gardens for a while and turn in early.'

'Make yourself at home,' Quinlan said easily.

She smiled at him gratefully and stood up. As she walked towards the door she heard Fiona mentioning their night out.

'I thought we would go into Dublin tonight, Quin. Have a few drinks at Bailey's and maybe go on to Leason Street.'

'Not tonight, Fiona. Matter of fact, I wouldn't mind an early night myself tonight.'

'Well, now you come to mention it...'

Holly closed the door on Fiona's throaty rejoinder. She bit down hard on the softness of her lip as she walked towards the front door. She didn't care what was going on between Quin and Fiona, she told herself furiously. She didn't give one damn.

The air was fresh outside after the heat of the day. A small breeze whispered in the trees and stirred the heavy pink heads of some late summer roses. Holly wandered a little way down the drive then on impulse turned towards the stables to see how Becky was settling in to her new home.

The chestnut mare seemed pleased to see her. She nuzzled her soft velvety nose against Holly and made small whinnying sounds of welcome. Holly stroked her neck. 'I'm pleased to see you too,' she said in a low, soothing tone.

The sound of a car's engine made Holly turn her head towards the drive. She recognised the Land Rover as Ross's and lifted her hand to wave at him. The car stopped midway up the drive and he wound the window down.

'Hello,' Holly called cheerfully. 'What brings you out here?'

'I was about to ask you the same question,' he answered drily.

He started the car again and parked it to one side of the drive then got out and walked across towards her.

He looked agitated; his face was red as if he had been running and his eyes moved over her in a sharply assessing way. 'I've just been over to your house. Flynn told me that you've moved in here.'

'That's right.' Holly continued to stroke Becky in a soothing, almost absent-minded way. 'Quin offered me a job.'

'Do you know what you're doing?' he demanded, and his voice had a harsh ring to it.

She looked at him, puzzled. 'It's a good job, Ross,' she said quietly. 'And you've got to admit they're scarce on the ground these days.'

'You're talking to *me* now, Holly. And you're not fooling me for a moment,' he said with a shake of his head. 'You know that you're in way over your head with Quinlan.'

'I've taken a job here, Ross,' Holly repeated firmly, and looked up at him with sparkling angry eyes. 'There's nothing else to it.'

He looked disbelieving. 'If you say so.'

'So, are you over here visiting Quin or me?' she asked now, striving to get things back on an even footing.

'You. I went over to your place to see if you'd like to come out for a drink.'

Holly hesitated. 'I don't know, Ross...' She pursed her lips thoughtfully. 'I suppose I would have to check with Quinlan. He might want me to listen out for Jamie. He hasn't been sleeping well lately.'

Ross lifted his eyebrows in an expression of disdain. 'Surely you have your evenings free? Or does Quinlan like to keep an extra-special close watch over you in the evening?'

'Don't be silly,' Holly muttered crossly.

Ross raked a hand through his hair and apologised immediately. 'Sorry, Hol... I shouldn't have said anything. It's none of my business. It's just that I'm worried about you.'

Holly smiled at him. 'Well, thank you for worrying about me,' she said softly. 'But I am all right, really I am.'

He nodded. 'So how about that drink? Just to prove to me that we are still friends.'

'I don't know...' She had been going to just turn in for the night, yet the thought of getting out and switching her mind away from Quinlan for a few hours was tempting.

'Good evening, Ross,' Quinlan's voice interrupted them as he strolled around the corner and came to stand next to them. 'I thought I recognised your car.' His eyes flicked from Holly towards the vet, taking in the closeness of their stance.

'Hello, Quinlan.' Ross greeted the other man with a pleasant smile. 'I've just popped over to see if I can tempt your new employee out for a drink, but she tells me that she has to check with you first.'

'Does she, now?' Quin drawled with a glimmer of humour in his tone. His eyes moved towards Holly and she felt herself colouring under the sparkle of his blue gaze. 'I thought you were tired and were turning in early,' he said in a dry tone. 'But, if you've changed your mind, then of course I will allow you to go out.'

The tinge of embarrassed colour in Holly's cheeks flamed to a tidal wave of angry vivid colour. She didn't care for his patronising tone at all. After all, who was he to *allow* her to go out? The nerve of the man! Nobody ordered her around like that.

'I was just concerned about Jamie,' she said frostily. 'I wanted to make sure there was someone listening out for him if I went out.'

'I'm sure we'll manage,' Quinlan murmured drolly.

'Then I will change my plans and gladly come out tonight, Ross.' She smiled up at Ross with forced enthusiasm.

Ross's expression became instantly brighter, if a little surprised. 'Great,' he said enthusiastically.

Holly gave Becky's neck a final pat. 'I'll just nip into the house and get my bag.'

'I'll show you around the stables while you're waiting, Ross,' Quinlan offered politely.

Holly flicked a glance up at him as she left them. Why was it that, for all his politeness, she couldn't help thinking that Quinlan Montgomery was far from pleased?

The local inn was very crowded but Ross managed to find them a seat in the corner. 'What would you like to drink, Holly?'

'Just an orange juice.' She watched as he made his way to the bar. Ross was really a very good-looking man, she thought absently. If only she could have fallen in love with him instead of Quinlan. She frowned and raked an impatient hand through her hair. Thoughts like that seemed to be getting increasingly aggravating recently. Why was she convincing herself that she loved Quin...why was she torturing herself with any romantic thoughts of that man when she knew they could never lead to anything?

'Hey, you're supposed to be here to have a good time,' Ross said lightly as he returned with their drinks. 'I've seen happier faces at a wake.'

'Thanks.' She smiled drolly.

'What's the matter?' He took a seat beside her.

'Nothing.' She shook her head, then changed the subject determinedly. She was not going to give Quin one more thought. 'How's Sinead?'

'Actually, a bit morose, which is most unlike my sister.' Ross took a sip of his pint. 'Must be something in the air recently, wouldn't you say?' he asked wryly.

'Must be,' Holly agreed lightly. For a moment she was half tempted to tell Ross what was the matter with his sister, but she had promised Sinead that she would say nothing so she held her tongue.

'What do you think about Flynn's decision to sell the farm?' he asked her curiously.

'I was furious at first.' Holly shrugged. 'But it is Flynn's life and if he isn't happy...' She trailed off for a moment. 'I hate the thought of him going to Australia,' she finished sadly.

Ross nodded. 'Maybe he'll change his mind.'

'Maybe...' Holly thought it was a big maybe.

The conversation turned to more general things and Holly felt herself starting to relax.

'It's amazing how time flies when you enjoy yourself,' Ross remarked as he came back from the bar with some more drinks. 'They've just called time. I hope Quin hasn't put a curfew on your stopping out late.'

Holly laughed. 'No, he's not quite that——' She broke off and put one hand across her mouth as a sudden terrible thought struck her.

'What is it?' Ross asked her, full of concern immediately.

'I haven't got a front-door key!' Holly exclaimed in distress. 'I can't get in.'

For a moment Ross smiled. 'Never mind, I'm sure Quin will wait up for you,' he murmured drily.

Holly shook her head. 'He said he was going to have an early night. Hell, what am I going to do? I hate the thought of trying to wake everyone in the house up.'

'You could always stay at my house tonight. I'll make sure that I have you back at Quin's first thing tomorrow.'

Holly frowned and shook her head. 'Thanks for the offer, Ross, but I couldn't.'

'I do have a spare bedroom if that's what's worrying you,' he said sardonically.

She smiled at him gratefully. 'Perhaps you would drive me back to Montgomery House first?' she asked him diplomatically. 'With a bit of luck someone will still be up. Maybe Mary—I believe she lives in now. If there's no one around then we can think about the alternatives.'

Ross shrugged. 'If that's what you want.'

They left their drinks and made their way out to the car park. It was pitch-dark outside now and the sky seemed to have clouded over for the first time in weeks.

'Looks as if the heatwave might be breaking,' Ross remarked as he looked up at the inky blackness of the sky. 'We could be in for a storm.'

Sure enough there were several flashes of lightning as they drove back to Montgomery House through the narrow country lanes, but there was no rain.

Holly's heart thudded nervously as they turned through the gates to Quin's house. She found herself praying that Mary would be around. She really dreaded the thought of waking Quin.

Ross stopped the car halfway down the drive as the house came into sight. It was in complete darkness.

'Damn!' Holly muttered in exasperation.

'I don't think you're going to get in without waking the whole house,' Ross remarked lightly.

The thought of dragging Quin from Fiona's bed made Holly's heart turn over.

'What's it to be... my house?' Ross looked over at her.

'Actually, I think it would be better if you dropped me home,' Holly said briskly. 'It's closer to here and I can get Flynn to drop me over first thing tomorrow morning.'

'You don't trust me?' Ross asked her, for a moment making no attempt to turn the car.

'It's not that, Ross. I just think it's more convenient to go home,' Holly hastily tried to assure him. She didn't want to upset Ross—they had been friends for too long—but there was a small part of her that was wary about going to his house. It wasn't that she thought he would pounce on her, but it might give him the wrong idea about her feelings towards him.

'Right, then, it's back to your old home.' Ross turned the car round with a shrug of his shoulders. 'I bet you didn't think you would be sleeping back there so soon. Quin will think I've persuaded you to quit his job.'

'I don't think so.' Holly dismissed that immediately.

'Or that I've seduced you into an evening of abandoned passion,' Ross continued with a dry note of humour in his tone now.

'Don't be ridiculous,' Holly retorted sharply.

Ross pulled his car through the gates to her old home. 'Is it so ridiculous a thought, Holly?' he asked softly, glancing across at her briefly.

She frowned at that. 'Ross, we've been friends a long time——'

'And we could never be anything else?' He pulled the car to a standstill by the front door.

She looked up at him. She couldn't see the expression on his face in the darkness but she could hear the hurt in his voice. 'Ross, please. You know I'm very fond of you.' She tried very hard to let the subject drop in a gentle way. 'Thank you for a lovely evening.'

He leaned across and kissed her cheek lightly. 'Goodnight, Holly. I'm sorry if I've embarrassed you.'

She shook her head. 'Of course you haven't.'

'I hope Quin isn't too angry with you tomorrow,' he finished lightly as she turned to open the car door.

'Of course he won't be angry.' She shook her head at the thought. 'As long as I'm there to do my work he won't care where I've been.'

'If you say so.' Ross's voice was dry, as if he knew differently.

CHAPTER NINE

HOLLY turned off the alarm clock and felt like turning over and going back to sleep. She buried her head in her pillow and for a moment she felt disorientated. She didn't know what day it was, or where she was. Then suddenly it all came back to her and she shot out of bed, her heart thumping. She had to get back to Quinlan's house before she was missed.

She glanced at the clock. It was nearly five; she had time to get dressed and have a drink of tea before Flynn came down. Pulling on the clothes she had worn last night, she brushed her hair hurriedly and went downstairs.

She was just filling the kettle when she heard steps on the stairs. 'It's only me, Flynn,' she called out just in case he thought that he had burglars.

He appeared in the doorway, still in his dressing-gown, his hair tousled and a bleary look of sleep on his face. 'Hell, you gave me a fright,' he muttered. 'What are you doing back here? I thought you were safely ensconced at Quin's place.'

'Nice to see you too, little brother,' Holly said with a grin. 'I forgot to get a key off Quin when I went out last night. So I was locked out and had to come home. Any chance of you dropping me back?' she finished with a hopeful smile.

Flynn shrugged. 'I might if you make me a nice cup of tea and put some rashers under the grill,' he said with a gleam in his eye.

'Some things never change,' Holly muttered. 'I was wondering how you would manage once I moved out.'

'I'm not doing so bad,' Flynn said, looking rather pleased with himself.

'Well, I haven't really gone yet,' Holly laughed. 'What did you have for dinner last night?'

'Oh... steak, medium-rare, jacket potato, cauliflower cheese, broccoli, washed down with Moët et Chandon.'

'I'm sure,' Holly laughed, not taking her brother's words seriously. Flynn was a notoriously bad cook and, left to his own devices, usually ended up with some kind of convenience food.

She turned towards the fridge and her eyes fell on the empty champagne bottle beside it. She frowned. 'I take it you were joking about last night's dinner?'

'Well, you take it wrong,' Flynn muttered glibly.

'So who cooked for you?' She turned to look at him.

'I don't know why you find it so hard to believe I can prepare a good dinner,' Flynn said with a grin.

'Because your sister knows you, Flynn Fitzgerald,' a woman's voice interrupted the conversation, and Sinead appeared in the kitchen doorway dressed in one of Holly's old dressing-gowns, her dark hair as tousled as Flynn's, her face flushed.

'Sinead!' To say that Holly was surprised was an understatement.

'You can close your mouth now, Holly,' Sinead laughed. 'Flynn and I have worked things out.' She put one arm around Flynn's waist and smiled up at him. 'I think your sister should be the first to know, don't you?'

Holly leaned back against the kitchen counter and listened in stunned amazement as Flynn announced in a proud and very happy voice, 'Sinead and I are going to get married.'

The next minute Holly was embracing them both, tears streaming down her face as happiness overflowed.

'Hey, this is supposed to be good news,' Flynn said gruffly. 'Let's open another bottle of champagne and have Buck's Fizz for breakfast.'

Flynn dropped Holly at the gates to Quinlan's house a little while later, on his way to take Sinead back into Dublin.

'I'm so pleased for you both,' Holly told them for the hundredth time as she opened the door to the car. 'I think you make a wonderful couple.'

Flynn nodded. He looked happier than Holly had ever seen him. 'So do I, Sis, so do I.'

Holly smiled and got out. Just before she closed the door, however, she couldn't resist asking the question that had been burning inside her since they had broken the good news. 'Does this mean you won't be going to Australia?'

For a moment there was indecision on Flynn's handsome face. 'We'll see,' he said. 'Sinead and I have to talk very seriously about it. Sinead has her business in Dublin to think about.'

Holly nodded, a ray of hope starting to build up inside her. 'Well, it's a big decision.' She smiled over at her friend. 'Ring me soon.'

'Oh, don't worry, I will.' Sinead grinned at her. 'I haven't heard all the low-down on you working for Quin yet.'

'There's nothing to hear,' Holly said firmly.

'Oh, no?' Sinead looked most disbelieving. 'I don't believe that for one moment. I reckon Quinlan Montgomery has quite a soft spot for you.'

'Rubbish.' Holly forced herself to laugh at the ridiculous statement. But there was a little part of her that couldn't help wishing what Sinead had said were true. She stood and waved as they drove off, then walked up the drive towards Quin's house with a lighter heart than she had had in weeks. Things weren't so bad. Flynn and Sinead were happy and they might not go to Australia.

The front door was unlocked and Holly practically waltzed into the hall, her eyes sparkling with happiness. She stopped short as she saw Quinlan standing by the hall table. There was an ominous look on the dark, handsome face.

'Where the hell have you been?' he demanded angrily.

For a moment Holly was taken aback by the tone of his voice and that look on his face. She frowned. 'I don't think you have any call to speak to me like that, Quin,' she murmured coolly.

His eyes raked over her appearance in a scathing manner. 'When you say that you're going out for a drink I don't expect you to be coming in with the milk in the morning,' he muttered caustically.

Fiona appeared in the doorway behind him. She was dressed in a beautiful cream linen suit, her hair sitting perfectly, a small smile playing around her red lips. 'I told you not to worry about her, Quin,' she purred throatily. 'I did tell you that she had probably decided to stay over at her boyfriend's house.'

Holly cringed at the implications in the woman's voice. 'For your information, I was locked out last night.' She angled her chin up firmly as she met Quinlan's eye. She didn't like the way he was looking at her. She had done nothing wrong, and certainly nothing that she should be ashamed of.

'I see.' For a moment she thought that he might drop the whole thing, but she was wrong. He turned to look across at Fiona, his manner very cold. 'I thought that I asked you to give Holly a front-door key.'

'I did.' The woman stared calmly over at Holly. 'I gave it to you when I showed you your room yesterday, don't you remember?'

For a second Holly was nonplussed. Fiona hadn't given her a key.

'I put it on the bedside table for you,' Fiona continued crisply. 'I said, "There's your key. Put it somewhere safe."'

Holly's colour heightened at such a whopping great lie. She shook her head. 'Fiona, you didn't give me a key.' Somehow she managed to keep her voice calm and steady.

The woman laughed. 'You obviously forgot it. I'm sure it's just where I left it in your room.' The woman shrugged. 'And what does it matter anyway? I'm sure you were more than pleased just to stay with your boyfriend.'

'I didn't stay with my boyfriend,' Holly grated drily. 'Not that it's any of your business. Now, if you will excuse me, I want to shower and change before I see to Jamie.' With an angry look at Quin she marched past him upstairs.

The first thing she noticed when she went back into her bedroom was a front-door key sitting on her bedside table. She picked it up thoughtfully. She knew very well that Fiona hadn't given it to her yesterday. What on earth was the woman playing at? With a sigh she slipped the key safely into her handbag. She was going to have to be very careful around Fiona Matthews. Obviously the woman was out to cause trouble.

'Holly, pass me that report on your desk, will you?' Quin's curt voice broke the silence in the office, making Holly jump.

Nervously she searched through the stack of papers he had left on her desk. 'Which report?' She glanced across at him and met the full glare of disapproving blue eyes.

'The report I asked you to finish yesterday,' he said drily.

'Oh.' Anxiously she searched through the papers again and much to her relief found what she was looking for. Quin made her so nervous sometimes that she could feel herself going to pieces. She wasn't sure if it was just her imagination, but he seemed very abrupt with her these days.

She got up from her chair and walked over to put the file on his desk, conscious of his eyes watching her every movement. Fridays were the worst day of the week because, instead of leaving her to get on with the office work alone as he did other mornings, he stayed to catch up on his paperwork, which meant that they were working opposite each other for several hours.

The days had slipped into a busy routine and Holly had been working at Montgomery House for over three weeks now. She enjoyed the work and Jamie was a sheer pleasure to look after, but she just wished that she could relax around Quinlan. She felt as if he was watching her all the time and finding fault with her. Yet she knew her work was fine.

She had reorganised the office for him and things now ran in a very efficient manner. She could always be relied on to know exactly where each file was and exactly what was in it. It was only when he glared at her as he had been doing this morning that she could feel her confidence starting to dwindle, and it was then that she was apt to make mistakes.

'Is it OK?' She watched now as he flicked his eyes over her neat typing.

'It'll do,' he murmured.

'Thanks.' Holly couldn't keep the sardonic note out of her voice. She had spent hours preparing that report on her old home for him. There were exact details on the running of Fitzgerald Farm, down to the very last detail of how much the electric bill was last quarter, and all he could say was that it would do!

He glanced up at her and for the first time in days smiled. 'You've done a good job, Holly,' he said gently.

'Thanks,' she repeated. She turned away from him and went to sit back at her desk. She didn't like it when he was abrupt with her, yet when he was nice to her it was somehow even worse. Her heart started to pound uncomfortably, her cheeks flushed with colour and she was completely at a loss for words.

She bent her head and went back to her typing, very much aware that he was still watching her. After a few moments she could stand it no longer and looked over at him curiously. 'Is something wrong?'

He smiled at her. 'No, on the contrary. I was just thinking that you've worked very hard over the last few weeks. You haven't had much time to relax and enjoy yourself.'

'I've enjoyed looking after Jamie.' She glanced back at her work and hoped he would do the same.

'You haven't been out with Ross recently,' he continued, a dry edge to his velvet-deep voice. 'I hope we haven't been working you so hard that your social life is suffering?'

Holly glanced up again, wondering if he was being sarcastic. 'Don't worry, if I want to go out I shall clear it with you first, and I will make sure I have my front-door key.' It was the first time that either had mentioned that episode and as soon as Holly had spoken the words she regretted it.

Quinlan glared at her in a very cold way. 'Your weekends are your own. I would just appreciate it if you would inform me if you intend to stay out all night with your boyfriends.'

Holly's face clouded over ominously. He made it sound as if she was sleeping around with all and sundry, and that was something she had never done. 'I told you that I spent that night at home,' she said frostily. 'Not with Ross.'

'I know what you told me.' His voice was acid-dry. 'But you really don't need to make excuses to me. Your life is your own.'

For one moment Holly felt like throwing something at his infuriating face. Then she shrugged. Why should she care if he chose to think the worst of her? 'You're right,' she murmured. 'It's my life.'

The silence that descended after that was stifling. Holly glared at the work in front of her, feeling completely wound up. No matter how she had told herself that she didn't care what Quinlan thought of her, deep down she cared a hell of a lot. She cared so much that she could feel tears welling up inside her.

It was a relief when Fiona brought in their mid-morning coffee. As much as Holly disliked the other woman, at least she lightened the atmosphere in the room.

Fiona put the tray down and smiled at Quinlan. 'Are you nearly finished in here?'

'Another half-hour should do it.' Quinlan reached for his coffee. 'Why?'

Fiona perched on the edge of his desk, hitching her black skirt up a little further as she made herself comfortable. Then she sent a pointed glance over towards Holly. 'I just wanted a few quiet words with you, Quin,' she murmured softly.

Holly was only too grateful to take the hint and leave them alone.

'You don't need to go, Holly,' Quinlan said quickly as she stood up.

'It's all right.' Holly picked up her bag. 'I could do with a few minutes of fresh air anyway.'

'I have to go to Dublin for a few days, darling, and I thought that now we have Holly to look after things here we could go together.' Holly closed the door on the rest of the woman's sentence, feeling rather sick inside.

She didn't care, she told herself fiercely as she walked around the gardens for a little while. She didn't care what Quin and Fiona did.

She waited until she had got her wayward emotions under firm control before going back to the office. Fiona was still sitting on top of Quin's desk and she was drinking the coffee that she had brought in for Holly.

'Sorry, Holly. I didn't think you wanted this,' she said with a shrug.

'I don't.' Holly sat back at her desk and busied herself putting new paper in the electric typewriter.

Fiona continued with her conversation to Quin. 'At least think about it, Quin, darling,' she purred as she finished the coffee and put the china cup back down on its saucer.

'I can't, Fiona.' Quinlan's voice was firm. 'I have a lot to do this weekend.'

Holly fought down a feeling of joy. Quin wasn't going away with Fiona for the weekend.

'Well, it's up to you, of course, but I think a break would do you good.' Fiona wasn't about to leave the subject, although Holly could tell that she was uncomfortable talking in front of her.

'You're probably right.' Quinlan put his coffee-cup back on the tray and turned his attention back to the papers in front of him. 'But unfortunately this is one of my busiest times.' There was a note of dismissal in his voice that didn't escape Holly's attention. She couldn't help smiling to herself as she started to type.

'We'll talk about it later, when you haven't so much on your mind,' Fiona murmured, standing up and collecting the tray.

'Fine,' Quinlan murmured, his tone distracted. 'Holly, could you type this up next? It's very important—I want to send it away by first post tomorrow morning.'

Holly started to stand up to get the file from him but he passed it to Fiona to hand it over.

'I know there's a lot of work there; do you think you'll manage it all today?' Quin asked anxiously.

'I'll try.' Holly took the heavy file from Fiona and smiled at the woman in a friendly way.

Her smile met a blank stare.

'Speak to you later,' Fiona murmured to Quinlan, and left the room.

After that the only sound in the room was the sound of Holly's typewriter, yet the silence was a strangely companionable one after the strain of the morning.

Quinlan stood up after another hour or so. 'I'm going down to my solicitor in the village, Hol...' he murmured. 'The sale of your brother's farm should be completed today.'

'I see.' Her fingers stilled at the typewriter. 'So you are now the proud new owner of Fitzgerald Farm?' She tried very hard to keep any emotion out of her voice, but it was hard. Fitzgerald Farm had been home to her all her life.

Quin glanced at his watch. 'I will be in about half an hour.'

Holly bent her head and started to type again. 'Well, I wish you luck with it,' she murmured.

He moved over towards her desk and reached out a hand to tip her head up towards him. 'Do you mean that?' he asked huskily.

She swallowed hard as she met the blue eyes she had come to love so much. 'I suppose I do,' she murmured.

He smiled at her and his fingers caressed the softness of her face in an almost absent way before he straightened. 'Perhaps we can have a drink tonight to celebrate, then?'

Holly's eyebrows lifted. 'Alone?' The word just seemed to slip out.

His lips twisted in a dry smile. 'Unless you're frightened of being alone with me?'

'Don't be silly. We're alone in here most mornings.' She tried very hard to keep her voice crisp and businesslike.

'Yes, but that's different, isn't it?' he drawled.

Holly felt her heart starting to pound at the intimate tone of his voice.

He moved towards the door. 'I'll pick up some champagne while I'm out.'

Holly found it very hard to concentrate after that. Quin was just being friendly, she told herself sternly. Just because he had suggested they had a drink together, it didn't mean he was romantically interested in her in any way. He was probably just trying to fill in some time, seeing as Fiona was going to Dublin for the weekend. With that sobering thought Holly managed to plough on with the report in front of her.

She didn't see Quin again until later in the afternoon when she returned back to the house after collecting Jamie from school. He was out on the drive helping Fiona to put some bags in her car.

'Where are you going, Aunty Fiona?' Jamie asked as he climbed out of Holly's car.

'Back to Dublin.' The woman's voice was clipped. Obviously she was not pleased to be leaving without Quinlan.

'Are you coming back?' Jamie asked, putting one hand on his hip and looking up at her with interest.

'Of course I'm coming back.' The woman glared down at the child. 'You're getting very cheeky, Jamie.'

'He was just curious.' Holly put her hand on Jamie's shoulder in an instinctively protective way.

Fiona turned shimmering eyes up to Holly and for a moment the full force of her resentment towards Holly showed very clearly. Then, surprisingly, the red lips curved in a smile. 'Have a good weekend, Holly.'

'Thanks.' For a moment Holly was taken aback at the sudden turn in the woman's attitude. 'You too.'

'Oh, I shall.' The woman turned and smiled at Quinlan. 'See you on Monday.'

Quin opened the car door for her. 'Drive carefully.'

The woman moved over and stood next to him. She looked very glamorous in a cherry-red suit, her blonde hair loose and gleaming gold in the sunlight. She reached up to kiss him and Holly averted her eyes.

'Bye, Aunty Fiona,' Jamie murmured.

'Bye, sweetheart.' The woman got into her car without so much as a glance at the child. 'See you Monday.'

As Fiona's car drove away Quinlan turned with a smile. 'Who would like to go for a ride?'

'Me... me,' Jamie called in delight.

'Right, well, go and run over to the stable—see if you can find one of the hands to saddle your pony for you.'

'Are you coming, Holly?' the child asked before rushing off.

Holly hesitated. She wanted to come, but she didn't want to intrude on Quinlan's time with his son. 'Well, I——'

'Of course she's coming,' Quinlan cut across her firmly. 'We'll ride over to our new property next door.'

'You got the keys, I take it?' Holly asked as they followed Jamie towards the stables.

'Yes, I did.' He reached into his pocket and brought out a bunch of keys, a smile of triumph on his face.

Holly smiled sadly. 'I suppose Fitzgerald Farm will now be called Montgomery Farm,' she murmured.

Quinlan shrugged. 'I haven't thought of a change of name yet.'

'Did you see Flynn this afternoon?' Holly made a determined effort to sound more cheerful.

'Yes, I did.' For a moment Quinlan hesitated and she had the distinct impression that he was going to say something else, then changed his mind as they arrived at the stables.

'Look, Dad, look, Holly,' Jamie called to them as he scrambled up on to his little pony with an ease born of practice.

'That's very good, Jamie,' Holly called out, genuinely impressed.

Quinlan smiled at her. 'Thanks,' he said softly.

She frowned. 'What are you thanking me for?'

'For being so good with my son.'

She shrugged, feeling embarrassed by the words and the way he was looking at her. 'I've told you I've enjoyed looking after him.'

'Even so, I do appreciate it.'

A stable-hand brought out his horse and Holly seized the opportunity to escape for a moment in search of Becky. She didn't want Quin's thanks for looking after his son, she wanted more...much, much more; she wanted to feel as if she belonged here, as if... She stopped her train of thought abruptly. She didn't belong here; she was an employee, nothing more.

The afternoon passed very pleasurably. They cantered over the fields in a carefree manner. Holly loved the feel of the fresh air blowing through her hair; it brought a healthy glow to her skin and she felt wonderful when they finally arrived at what had once been her home. Her exhilaration died, however, when she looked around the farmyard. Everything seemed strangely quiet; the farm had a deserted feel about it. Yet it could only have been this morning that Flynn had left.

'You all right, Holly?' Quinlan asked her as he noticed the look on her face.

She nodded, but her heart was starting to beat in a very painful way in her chest. It was such a strange feeling knowing that this was no longer her home. It was the end of an era, the end of the ties that had kept this farm in her family back over the generations.

Quinlan dismounted and took out the keys to open the front door.

'Coming inside?' He looked up at her and she shook her head.

'No. I think I'll be getting back now if you don't mind.'

'OK.' His voice was gentle. 'I'll see you back home.'

'Back home'. The words echoed in Holly's head as she turned to ride back on her own. When the magnificent house came into view across the fields she pulled Becky up for a moment while she sat staring at it.

Montgomery House was beautiful, but it wasn't her home, not really. If Fiona married Quinlan her days at the house would be numbered, she knew that with certainty. Fiona would see to it that she left and really she didn't think she would want to stay, not with the way she felt towards Quinlan. It would be unbearable to look at him and know that he was another woman's husband. The mere thought was enough to start tears shimmering in her eyes.

Annoyed with herself, Holly urged Becky on again. What on earth was wrong with her? she wondered miserably. It must have been the trip to her old farm. Somehow the knowledge that Quinlan was buying it had remained like a hazy blur inside her until she was faced with the reality, and then all the emotions had suddenly taken forceful shape once more.

Holly was subdued for the rest of the day. Dinner with Jamie and Quinlan should have been enjoyable, but she couldn't rid herself of the sad feelings inside. It was so nice to listen to Jamie chatter and to laugh at his jokes but when she met Quinlan's eyes across the table she was struck with the intimacy of it all. She was becoming too attached to Jamie and it was dangerous. Just as it was dangerous to like the feeling of them as a small family around this table. It was unreal. They were not a family and her future here was very uncertain.

'You all right, Holly?' Quinlan asked after Jamie was safely tucked up in bed and it was just the two of them in the lounge.

'Yes, of course.' Holly couldn't quite bring herself to meet his eyes but instead gazed into the bright flickering flames of the fire. 'The evenings are getting cooler now, aren't they?' she asked in an attempt to make small talk.

He came and sat down next to her on the settee. 'What's the matter?' Gently he placed a hand under her chin and turned her head so that he could look into her eyes.

She shrugged. 'I don't know; maybe it's just knowing that Fitzgerald Farm is no longer anything to do with me,' she murmured, wishing that he would remove his hand. The touch of his skin next to hers made a shiver race down her spine.

'Of course it has something to do with you,' he said firmly. 'I'll see to that.' He grinned at her. 'Don't worry, you'll know everything there is to know about the running of that farm. You'll probably be typing up a report on it at the end of every month.'

She smiled. 'I appreciate your trying to cheer me up, Quinlan,' she said softly.

'Who said I was trying to cheer you up?' he asked humorously. 'You'll be working very hard for me where that farm is concerned. I'll be relying a lot on your knowledge of the place in these first few months.'

She nodded, but she was hardly listening, her mind running on different lines. 'Did you speak with Flynn today?' she asked suddenly.

'Yes.' He hesitated before continuing, 'He told me that he's planning to marry Sinead.'

Holly nodded. 'He's moved into Dublin to be nearer to her.'

'He also told me that you had spent the night at the farm when you were locked out of here,' Quinlan continued crisply.

She nodded. 'I told you that.'

'I know and I'm sorry that I doubted your word.'

The softness of his words surprised her. She frowned, trying desperately not to let his gentle mood get to her wayward emotions. 'It doesn't matter,' she said, then crisply changed the subject. 'I was wondering if by any chance you had managed to talk to Flynn about his going to Australia?'

Quinlan hesitated. 'As a matter of fact I did mention it today. We went for a drink after the completion of the sale.'

'And?' Holly looked at him hopefully. She had been worrying more and more recently about her brother leaving, especially as Sinead had been unusually unforthcoming about their plans recently.

Quin's gaze moved over the pallor of her skin and the anxious light in her eyes and shook his head. 'I hate to be the one to break the news to you, Holly,' he said gently, 'but——'

'No!' Holly cut across him in a stunned tone. 'No.' She shook her head, trying to reject the news, as if somehow by doing so she could change it.

'I'm sorry.' He reached for her hand. 'I tried to change his mind, even offered him a job as manager on the farm.'

Holly bit down sharply on her lip and her eyes brimmed with simmering tears.

'Sorry, Quinlan.' Her voice was strained with the effort of trying not to cry. She didn't want to cry in front of him, didn't want to lower those barriers and let him see her in such a vulnerable state. 'Sorry, you'll have to excuse me.' She pulled her hand away from his and got sharply to her feet to run from the room.

Only when she was in the sanctuary of her own room did she allow the floodgates to open. She sat on the edge of her bed and wept as she hadn't wept since the death of her parents.

She didn't hear the knock on her door, therefore she was startled when Quinlan spoke softly in the silence of her room.

'Don't cry, Holly. I hate to see you like this.'

'Then go away,' she murmured miserably. 'Please, Quinlan, leave me alone for a while.'

He ignored those words completely and instead sat down next to her.

'Come on, it's not the end of the world. Anything could happen yet. They might not like Australia; they might come home again.'

Holly shook her head. 'I'll probably never see him again.' She buried her head in her hands, embarrassed that he should see her like this, but too full of grief to be able to pull herself together.

'Now you're being silly.' Suddenly he pulled her into his arms. 'Of course you'll see him again. There are planes to Australia,' he joked gently, and stroked her hair.

'Stop it, Quin.' Her voice held a note of panic. Suddenly she was very aware of how close they were, the wonderful feeling of his strong arms around her, the smell of his cologne. She pushed at him, desperately struggling for control.

'Here.' He moved away for a moment to hand her a handkerchief from his pocket. 'Come on, cheer up. I hate to see you cry.'

She blew her nose furiously. 'And I hate you to see me crying,' she said fiercely.

He smiled at her. His blue eyes were so gentle, so...understanding somehow. Holly could feel her heart pumping. It had felt so wonderful in his arms, so safe— as if when she was close to him he could make everything better. A ridiculous notion, yet the feeling intensified as she looked up at him.

'Hold me, Quinlan.' She was barely aware that she had spoken the words out loud; for a moment they seemed to be coming from somewhere deep within her soul. 'Hold me.'

CHAPTER TEN

AFTERWARDS Holly wasn't sure just how it happened. One moment she was being held in Quinlan's arms and he was making low, soothing noises as he stroked her hair, the next he was kissing her passionately.

His lips trailed a heated path over the smooth, damp contours of her face until he found her lips, and then he took possession of them with such force that for a moment Holly felt dizzy with the sheer intensity of the emotions he was unleashing inside her. She clung to him weakly, hardly daring to believe what was happening to her. It was like a dream, a wonderful, sensational dream, and she was terrified that at any moment she would wake up.

'Holly, sweetheart.' His voice was thick with desire as he lifted his head for a moment to look at her. 'I want you so much.'

For some crazy reason that made her start to cry again.

Gently he kissed her tears away. 'Don't cry, Holly, I can't bear it.' He whispered the words huskily against her ear. His hands found the buttons on the front of her blouse and she could feel him unfastening them slowly.

For a moment she was so stunned that she just lay completely still in his arms. Then she felt his hands against her naked skin, stroking, soothing, and a wave of red-hot desire swept through her.

'Quinlan.' She whispered his name, and reached her hands up to cling to him as he lowered her back so that she was lying on the bed.

His lips trailed down the sensitive column of her neck and then lower to her breasts. She moaned with pleasure, raking her hands through the thick darkness of his hair, her mind blank of everything except the desire he was stirring up inside her.

He lifted his head and smiled down at her, his eyes raking over the soft curves of her young body, the spill of auburn hair against the pale satin covers of the bed, the luminous glow of her skin, flushed with his lovemaking. 'You are so beautiful,' he murmured huskily.

She smiled, and for a brief moment happiness exploded inside her. He thought she was beautiful; he had called her sweetheart . . . maybe, just maybe he loved her as much as she loved him.

'I want to make love to you, Holly.' He said the words in a low, deep voice, and as he spoke he traced the curve of her breast with one infinitely gentle finger, sending shivers of pleasure racing through her. 'Right at this moment I want you more than I've ever wanted any woman.'

What about Fiona? The question broke into her thoughts abrasively. Did he say the same thing to her before they made love? The cold question was like ice in her heart and suddenly the enormity of what was happening struck her terribly. She was about to make love with another woman's fiancé. Quinlan wanted to marry Fiona, not her; she would just be a pleasant distraction for one night. Afterwards there would be no place in this house for her. She would have lost her home, her job and the respect of the only man she had ever really loved.

Quinlan reached for her and she moved before he could touch her, before her strength of mind deserted her.

'No, Quinlan.' Her voice was strained. 'This . . . this just isn't right. She was hastily doing up the buttons on her blouse now, her fingers trembling so much that it seemed to be taking forever. 'I'm sorry... I——'

'For heavens sake, Holly,' he cut across her impatiently. 'What's wrong? I thought you wanted me. I could have sworn a few moments ago that your body was crying out for my touch, for my lips.'

Holly's face flamed crimson red with mortification. Had she led him on? The mere thought made her pride rebel forcibly. 'I'm sorry if I gave you the wrong impression.' Somehow she managed to look him straight in the eye. They were beautiful eyes, so blue, so intense that she felt lost in them for a moment and her voice faltered and came to a halt.

'You certainly managed to do that all right.' His voice was arid. 'I could have sworn...' His voice trailed off and he raked a hand through his dark hair. 'I'm sorry, Holly, I had no right to touch you the way I did.' His voice was gruff. 'I guess I just got carried away... you are a very beautiful woman... we are both consenting adults and I——'

'And you thought that we could just have a one-night fling,' Holly cut across him furiously, her eyes glittering brightly as anger took her over. His apology was like a whiplash across raw skin. His kiss had raised so many hopes that she previously hadn't dared to hope... Now they lay smashed to pieces and her heart was so heavy that it actually felt painful and tight. How naïvely stupid to let herself actually think that he felt anything for her. 'Well, I'm very sorry, Quinlan, but I wouldn't dream of having a one-night fling with you.'

For a moment he looked angry. It was the first time that she had ever seen him look so blazingly mad and for one instant she was afraid.

'Good old Fitzgerald family honour to the rescue, is that it, Holly?' he drawled sardonically. 'Kiss a

Montgomery and immediately think you'll be damned for all time.'

She bit down hard on her lip and fought to remain calm. 'I'm sorry to disappoint you, Quinlan, but my refusal has nothing to do with family honour. I just happen to think that two-timing someone is reprehensible. I have never done anything underhand or deceitful in my life, and I don't intend to start now.'

For a moment he just stared at her; his eyes were cold and they glittered furiously. 'Highly commendable,' he murmured at last, a jeering note in his voice. 'It's just a pity your high moral codes didn't click into place before you started to kiss me with such fierce abandon.' With that he calmly stood up and walked out of the room.

Holly buried her head in her hands, her face burning with a mixture of humiliation and anger, and in between those fierce emotions the tears were rolling down her cheeks. How dared he speak to her like that? He was the one who had contemplated two-timing Fiona, yet he made it sound as if she was the one who had behaved dishonourably.

She had wanted him, though... the thought stole into her mind. If wanting someone was a crime then she was very, very guilty. And she had kissed him passionately. A wave of red-hot heat seared her violently. She loved Quinlan Montgomery with all her heart and the knowledge that he would never return her love, that he belonged to another woman, was almost more than she could bear. With a strangled sob she flung herself facedown on the bed and wept bitter, bitter tears.

Somehow Holly must have fell into a deeply exhausted sleep, because when she stirred again the light was filtering through the windows. She sat up feeling stiff and uncomfortable and glanced at her watch. It was nearly seven in the morning! How could she have slept so soundly after what had happened?

Wearily she got up from the bed. The first thing she saw was her reflection in the mirror. She looked terrible. Her face was swollen with tears and she was still wearing her clothes from yesterday. Slowly she made her way through to the bathroom and turned on the shower before stripping off her clothes. She felt a little better after she had stood under the forceful jet of water. Then she returned to her room and stood surveying the contents of her wardrobe.

How was she going to be able to face Quinlan today? That thought was foremost in her mind. She had made such a fool of herself yesterday, had allowed him to kiss her, caress her in the most intimate way, had actually encouraged his caresses. Her face flushed scarlet as the memories returned.

Had she thrown herself at him? For the life of her she couldn't think just how it had gone so far. All she knew was that it was wrong. Quinlan was going to marry another woman; he had just been amusing himself with her last night. She pushed a distraught hand through her hair. Last night had made her position in this house unbearable. She couldn't stay on... not now.

With shaking hands she picked out a cream skirt and top and dressed quickly. She would have to go down and face Quinlan, would have to put a brave face on things for the time being. She would manage it just as long as Quinlan didn't guess her true feelings for him; that would be the last straw. Her pride was the only thing she had left, and she intended to hang on to that at all costs.

She applied her make-up carefully to hide the ravages of her face and then, with a last glance in the mirror to make sure that she looked cool and composed, she went downstairs.

She wasn't really surprised to find Quinlan already in his office. He often went in there early to sort through paperwork before going out on the farm. She didn't know what reaction to expect from him after last night, but it certainly wasn't the one she got.

He was seated in his leather chair going through the drawers of his desk in a brisk way. He glanced up at her as she came into the room and there was no softening of his stern expression as his eyes swept over her.

'I'm looking for that report on the stud farm. I thought I asked you to finish typing it up for me yesterday?' he demanded crisply.

Holly felt herself flinch at his tone, at the cold gleam in those blue eyes. He despised her; she could see it there on his lean, attractive features. Last night he had been playing with her, had enjoyed the challenge of trying to get her into bed. Today in the plain light of morning he wanted to forget the incident, and he probably wanted her as far away from him as possible.

Somehow she kept her head up and her voice steady. 'I did.' She walked across to her desk, conscious that he was watching her every movement. 'It's here.'

She opened her top drawer and took out the file. She had worked very hard yesterday to finish the report for him and she was extremely glad now that she had put so much extra effort in. Quinlan was obviously looking for some excuse to vent his displeasure on her. She opened the folder and took out the top pages, then frowned. The folder only contained half of the report!

'That's strange.' She spoke in a low voice, almost to herself. 'I finished the report and I'm sure I put it all in here.'

'Well, it doesn't seem to be there, does it?' Quinlan's voice was dry and it grated on Holly's raw nerves.

'Well, I can assure you that it was here yesterday,' she told him firmly.

'So why isn't it there now?' One dark eyebrow lifted sardonically.

'Are you calling me a liar?' She glared across at him, her dark eyes shimmering with furious resentment. How dared he speak to her like that?

'No... I'm asking a simple question.' His voice was calm and yet there was an undercurrent in it that tore at Holly's heart. He didn't believe her... he thought that she hadn't bothered to finish her work yesterday and that she was lying to cover up. It was the very last straw.

'I did tell you that the report was very important,' he continued wryly. 'I'd expected better from you, Holly.'

Holly couldn't believe what she was hearing. 'I finished the report and I put it right here.' She shook the folder at him. 'Someone has obviously taken it... maybe someone who is looking for an excuse to get rid of me...?' She glared at him coldly. 'But I can assure you that you need no excuse to get rid of me, Quinlan, because I'm going anyway. You have my resignation.' With that she walked coolly and calmly from the room.

She was shaking when she got back to her bedroom. She couldn't believe that Quinlan would stoop so low as to do something like that! If he wanted to sack her, he need not have gone to such lengths; all he had to do was tell her. She was only here on trial anyway and the month was up this weekend.

Her hands were trembling so much from the shock and fury of it all that she could hardly fold her clothes as she started to put them into her suitcase. In the end she just threw everything in and closed the lid with such force that she had no problem locking it.

A knock on the door distracted her from clearing the dressing-table. She didn't answer it. She knew it was Quinlan and she had nothing more to say to him.

'For heaven's sake, Holly.' He opened the door anyway and stood inside. 'This is ridiculous; I never meant to suggest that you were fired.'

She glared around at him. 'Nobody calls me a liar,' she told him coldly.

'I believe those were your words, not mine,' he said calmly.

She shrugged. 'But that's what you were implying.'

'No, I wasn't.'

For a moment she looked at him. He looked tired. His attractive face was carved into a stern, almost bleak expression. 'Come downstairs and we'll discuss this like adults,' he said gently.

Holly hesitated. In ordinary circumstances she would have done just that, but these were no ordinary circumstances. Her emotions were too tangled up with this man for her to be able to think clearly and rationally. She loved him so much that just looking at him made her whole body burn and ache with the need to go into his arms.

She shook her head. 'I can't, Quinlan. I really think that it's best I leave.' She picked up her case and walked towards him, just leaving the contents of the dressing-table behind.

He didn't move out of her way and she was forced to stop in front of him. 'Please, Quinlan. I want to leave.' How she managed to say those words she didn't know.

'I don't want you to leave.' He spoke calmly and rationally. 'And I certainly didn't invent any excuse to get rid of you.'

Holly bit down on her lip. She didn't want him to say anything else. It was easier to leave if she believed the worst of him, although deep in her heart she knew Quinlan would not have taken the report as an excuse to get rid of her... he just wasn't that kind of a man. 'I know...' she said slowly and then looked up at him. 'But I want to go, Quinlan; surely you know that I can't stay here now.'

He was silent for a moment. 'You mean because of last night?'

'Oh, for heaven's sake, of course.' She tried to push past him and that was a grim mistake because he caught hold of her and held her so closely that her heart seemed to stand still for a moment.

'Where will you go?' His voice was dry and almost raw.

'I don't know.' She pushed at him with a firm hand. 'Please, let me go.' Her voice caught on a sob and he immediately moved out of her way.

Tears weren't far away as she moved downstairs. He made no move to follow, just stood watching her from the top of the stairway.

'Goodbye, Quinlan.' She looked around at him before going out.

He made no reply. His blue eyes were grim, the strong, rugged features closed somehow.

Holly could hardly see as she drove down the long driveway. Her eyes were blurred with bitter tears. She loved Quinlan so much, and Jamie... Poor Jamie, he would wonder where she was... As soon as she got out of the driveway she pulled the car into the side of the road and gave in to the tears. She had done the right thing, she told herself firmly. It was better that she make the break now before Quinlan married Fiona.

CHAPTER ELEVEN

'So, WHAT did you think of my dress?' Sinead asked brightly.

'You looked fabulous in it, and you know it.' Holly smiled.

'And what about the bridesmaid dress for you—have you decided which one you like?' Sinead asked anxiously.

Holly shrugged. 'Any except the pink one. I'll leave it up to you.'

Sinead frowned. 'OK, I'll take another look at them in my lunch-hour tomorrow.'

Holly watched her friend making a quick note of that on the list in front of her. They were sitting in Bewley's café having a coffee together after a very gruelling day shopping for Sinead's wedding. Holly was exhausted and it wasn't just from the busy Dublin streets. She didn't seem able to sleep these days. Her mind was troubled all the time with thoughts of Quinlan...worries about Jamie. She missed them both so much that it was like a constant dull ache inside her.

Sinead looked up and caught the stricken expression on her friend's face. 'Holly, are you all right?' She was immediately filled with concern.

'Yes, of course.' Holly hid her feelings away behind a falsely bright smile. The last thing she wanted was to let her friend know how troubled she was. Sinead had enough on her plate with trying to organise her wedding.

For a moment Sinead contemplated her friend silently. Holly had lost a lot of weight during the three weeks she had been living back in Dublin and her eyes were like huge dark smudges in the pallor of her face. 'Come on, Holly. I can see that you're not yourself,' Sinead said quietly. 'Would you like to talk about it?'

Holly shook her head. She wasn't up to talking about Quinlan; at the mere thought of mentioning his name she felt like dissolving into tears.

'I'm all right, Sinead. Really I am. It's just taking me a bit longer to settle back into the city than I thought, that's all.'

Sinead pursed her lips and looked as if she didn't believe a word. 'I had to go down to Greystones yesterday,' she said after a moment's hesitation. 'I saw Ross. He wanted me to give him your new address.'

'You didn't, did you?' Holly asked anxiously.

'No.' Sinead shook her head. 'But it was a bit difficult trying to explain to him why not. He was a little hurt.'

Holly grimaced. 'I'm sorry, Sinead, it's just that I need some space on my own at the moment. I'm just not up to company.'

Sinead nodded and then hesitated for a moment before continuing. 'Ross said that Quinlan came up to his house looking for you.'

For a moment Holly's heart stood still.

'He said that you've left some stuff at his house,' Sinead continued.

'Oh.' Holly's heart felt as if it had fallen into a deep, bottomless black hole. What did she expect? she asked herself crossly. Of course Quinlan wasn't missing her; of course he wasn't interested in where she was.

'Quin seemed to be under the impression that you were staying with Ross,' Sinead continued curiously. 'I wonder whatever gave him that idea?'

Holly shrugged. She didn't want to have this conversation. She wanted so much to forget about Quinlan and to start living her life again with some enthusiasm. 'Shall we go, Sinead?' Determinedly she changed the subject and glanced at her watch. 'I want to pick up a few groceries on the way back to my flat.'

Sinead agreed with a nod and finished her coffee. 'Why don't you come and have dinner with Flynn and me tonight?' she asked as they made their way back out on to Grafton Street.

'It's nice of you, but I think I'll just try and have an early night tonight,' Holly said with a wan smile.

'OK, but ring me in the morning.' Sinead came to a standstill as they reached the bottom of the street. Both girls had to go in opposite directions from there. For a moment Sinead hesitated. She was worried about her friend and she didn't really like leaving her when she looked so unhappy. 'Are you sure you don't want to come back to our flat? I can easily make dinner for three,' she said with a persuasive lilt in her voice.

'Thank you, Sinead.' Holly smiled gratefully. 'I'll take you up on the offer another time.'

'Be sure you do,' Sinead said sternly. 'And be sure to eat a proper dinner this evening.'

Holly smiled and embraced her friend warmly. She was going to miss Sinead when she left for Australia after the wedding. Sinead and Flynn had been wonderful to her since she had moved back to the city. She blinked back an errant tear as she straightened. 'Right. I'll speak to you tomorrow,' she said briskly and turned to walk away.

It was a golden October day. The sky was vivid blue and clear and the air was crisp with the promise of frost that night. Holly snuggled closer into her thick wool coat and set off at a brisk pace down beside Trinity College. It was a good half-hour walk to her flat but she quite enjoyed the exercise. Hopefully it would put some colour back into her cheeks, she thought, trying to inject a spring into her step.

She stopped at the corner shop near her flat and stocked up with milk and bread and a few other necessities and then struggled across the road with them.

Her flat was on the top floor of an old Georgian house. It was a rather stylish residence, although the interior had seen better days.

As Holly walked across the wide hallway her landlady opened her door at the bottom of the stairs.

'Ah, Miss Fitzgerald.' The woman was beaming all over her face. 'Your fiancé is here. He has been waiting for over an hour for you.'

'My fiancé?' For a moment Holly stared at the woman as if she had gone mad. 'No, I think you've got that wrong. You mean my brother,' Holly corrected her, thinking that Flynn had taken it upon himself to come and try and persuade her to come back with him for tea.

'Oh...' The woman shook her head and looked perplexed. 'Well, I hope it's all right, but I let him go up and wait for you in your flat.'

Holly nodded. 'Yes, fine, thank you.' Briskly she made her way upstairs and then fiddled with her key to get it in the lock of her door.

It swung open before she had a chance to turn it and a strong pair of arms took her shopping bags from her.

'Thanks, Flynn—I...' Holly trailed off and stared at the man who was standing in front of her with amazed disbelief. 'Quin! What on earth are you doing here?' It was amazing how calm her voice sounded considering the trembling inside her body. Her knees felt weak just at the very sight of him.

He gave a lop-sided smile. 'I hope you don't mind but I told your landlady that I was your fiancé. It was the only excuse I could think of to get her to let me in.'

'No, I don't mind.' Holly shook her head. She had dreamt a few times that Quinlan came looking for her and she was afraid that at any moment she was going to wake up, that this was just another one of those dreams that melted away into cruel reality when the daylight hours descended.

She watched as he put her bags down on a nearby chair. He looked real enough. He was wearing a pair of black denim jeans and a thick blue jumper that exactly matched the deep shade of his eyes. As he turned to look at her she felt herself grow hot inside. This had to be a dream.

'So how are you?' he asked calmly, his blue eyes raking over her with an intensity that was most unnerving.

Holly shook her head and completely ignored that question. 'Quinlan, what are you doing here?' she asked in a strained voice. 'And how did you know where to find me?'

'Oh, a desperate man can be quite resourceful,' he drawled with a teasing note in his voice. Yet behind the humour Holly sensed that he was tense. There was a tired look about him and the eyes that watched her were serious.

'Is everything all right with Jamie?' Suddenly she panicked as the thought crossed her mind that he had come to tell her something awful had happened.

'Jamie is fine,' Quinlan murmured soothingly. 'The only thing wrong is that he misses you. We both do.'

For a second Holly had to fight hard not to cry. She had often wished that Quinlan would come and say that to her. Only she had wanted him to mean it in a romantic sense, which was utterly ridiculous. Quinlan only meant that he missed her as a boss missed a good employee.

She busied herself taking off her coat and tried not to meet his eyes as she spoke. 'I miss Jamie as well. But I'm sorry, Quin, I can't come back to work for you.'

'I don't want you to come back to work for me,' he said briskly.

'Oh.' Feeling very foolish now, Holly moved to hang up her coat. 'So why are you here?' She forced herself to turn and look at him, running her hands down her fine angora sweater in a nervous way.

'God, Holly, you've lost far too much weight.' For a moment his attention was distracted as his eyes swiftly took in her figure. 'Are you all right?'

'Of course I'm all right,' she snapped crossly. 'I've been on a diet.' It was a blatant lie but she didn't want him to know that she had been so upset since leaving him that she hadn't been able to eat.

'You don't need to diet, you were perfect the way you were,' he said huskily.

Holly swallowed hard. 'Don't be nice to me, Quinlan,' she snapped suddenly. 'I can't bear it.'

He frowned at that. 'That's a new one on me,' he drawled. 'I thought you used to complain that I wasn't "nice" enough.'

She swept a trembling hand through her hair. 'Just say whatever it is you've come to say and leave me alone.' Her dark eyes watched him cautiously as he crossed the room to stand beside her.

'Well——' he reached out a hand and tipped her chin so that she was forced to look directly into his eyes '—I came to tell you that we miss you and I want you to come home with me.'

She stared up at him, bewilderment clear in her beautiful eyes. 'I... I don't understand. I——'

'I love you, Holly,' he murmured. 'I love you and I miss you like crazy.'

Tears sparkled in Holly's eyes. This couldn't be happening; any moment now she was going to wake up.

'Holly, please.' For the first time since Holly had known Quin she heard a note of deep anxiety in his voice. 'Ever since I allowed you to walk out of my door I've been as miserable as hell. I even went around to Ross and created a scene, demanding to see you.'

Holly shook her head; she felt numb inside and yet she was trembling like a small frightened child. 'If this is some kind of a joke, Quin, then I——'

'I've never been more serious in my life.' He caught hold of her shoulders and stared deep into her face. 'When you walked out on me I thought that you were in love with Ross, that you were going to him. You don't know what that did to me, Holly. It tore me apart. Then when Ross told me that you were in love with me——'

'Ross told you that!' Holly's face flushed a deep crimson red.

He nodded. 'Please, Holly, tell me that you love me. I've been going out of my mind with wanting you.'

A tiny tear trickled down her face. 'I do love you, Quin,' she murmured in a low voice. 'And I've missed you too.'

She didn't get to say anything after that for a long time. Quinlan wrapped her in his arms and his lips found hers in a hungry kiss.

Holly clung to him weakly when he finally lifted his head. 'I've dreamt of this moment for so long that I can hardly believe it's happening,' he murmured huskily. 'I love you so much, Holly Fitzgerald.'

'And I thought you were in love with Fiona,' Holly said in a shaking voice. Her heart was hammering so loudly against her breast that it felt almost painful.

'Fiona?' For a moment he looked startled. 'Fiona is Jamie's aunt...nothing more.'

'But I thought that you wanted to marry her...I thought that——'

'When you talked about two-timing somebody that night when we were kissing, you were talking about Fiona?' he cut across her roughly.

'Well, yes, I——'

'I thought you meant Ross,' he grated harshly. 'There has never been anything between Fiona and me. She very kindly offered to come down for the summer when I was short of a childminder but that's as far as it goes.'

'But I thought that you were involved...' Holly trailed off, her cheeks growing hot.

'The idea is totally ridiculous. In fact I was desperate to try and get her out of the house after the first couple of weeks. The woman drove me demented and she was hopeless with Jamie. Wanted to put the child in boarding-school, for heaven's sake.'

'Yes, but you considered that yourself at one point.'

'Only as a ruse to make you come and work for me.' He grinned. 'It worked, too.'

'You devious so-and-so.' She aimed a playful punch at him and he caught her arm and swung her up into the warmth of his arms.

'It was a means to an end... and, talking of endings, you know I did find the end of that report you typed for me.'

'You did?' She looked at him in surprise. 'Where was it?'

'Mary found it in Fiona's bedroom when she was tidying up,' Quin said drily. 'I presume it was another episode like the front-door key.'

'You knew about that?' she asked in surprise.

'I had my suspicions.' He smiled down at her. 'But at the time I was just so damn jealous that you had spent the night with Ross...'

'There has never been anything between Ross and me. We're just very good friends,' she told him quickly.

'So he told me, albeit a little grudgingly.' Quin grinned. 'You can't blame me for being jealous, though. You and Ross were always an item. Always together.'

'Only because Sinead is my closest friend.'

'If you don't mind, I would like to claim that position now,' Quin said with a laughing glint in his eye. 'I want to be your closest friend, your lover, your husband.'

For a moment Holly's heart seemed to miss a beat. 'Is that a proposal of marriage?' she asked breathlessly.

'Why else do you think I'm here?' he growled in a low, husky tone before claiming her lips again.

His kiss was warm and tender this time and it made Holly feel dizzy with longing.

'Was that a yes?' he murmured huskily as he lifted his head.

'It certainly was... on all three counts,' she whispered happily.

He lifted her up at that and carried her to the settee where they sat and kissed for quite some time.

'I guess this is well and truly the end of the Fitzgerald-Montgomery feud,' he said with a grin.

'I reckon it is,' she said simply. 'Because I love you, Quin, with all my heart.'

He smiled. 'You know, I don't think I've ever felt so happy,' he murmured wondrously. 'I don't think I've ever felt love so deeply, so intensely.'

She looked at him and for a brief moment there was sadness in her eyes. 'I'm sure you have, Quinlan,' she murmured.

'You mean with Camilla?' he said sadly. 'Yes, I loved Camilla. She was my childhood sweetheart. We grew up together, we had fun together, but I never really planned on marrying her.' For a moment he was silent, his thoughts far away, his face sad. 'I was about to end our relationship when she told me she was dying... and the doctors had given her a year at most.'

'Oh, Quinlan...' Holly's voice was filled with anguish.

'Yes, it was very traumatic. Poor Camilla.' Quinlan pulled himself together and smiled at Holly. 'But she was a brave kid. She said her only regrets were that she didn't have time to marry me or have a family.'

'So you married her,' Holly whispered in a strained voice.

'Straight away.' He nodded. 'And we were happy. We had two wonderful years, not one, and of course we had Jamie. I don't have any regrets about that marriage. Camilla was a wonderful girl.'

'Oh, Quinlan.' Tears streamed down Holly's face.

'Hey, you're not supposed to be crying.' Quinlan kissed her cheeks and wiped away the tears. 'That's all in the past, and I can assure you that I did make Camilla happy.'

'Knowing you, I'm sure you did.' Holly sniffed back the tears. 'It's just so sad.'

He nodded. 'But we had some happy times together, and that's a lot more than some people have.' He caressed her face soothingly. 'And I know we have a lot of happy times ahead of us.'

She nodded and reached up to kiss him. 'I love you, Quin, and I love Jamie too. I'll try my hardest to make you both happy.'

He smiled at that. 'Just be yourself, Holly. Because you are all I've ever wished for.'

MILLS & BOON

Proudly present...

This is a remarkable achievement for a writer who had her first Mills & Boon novel published in 1973. Some six million words later and with sales around the world, her novels continue to be popular with romance fans everywhere.

Her centenary romance *'VAMPIRE LOVER'* is a suspense-filled story of dark desires and tangled emotions—Charlotte Lamb at her very best.

Published: June 1994   Price: £1.90

Available from WH Smith, John Menzies, Volume One, Forbuoys, Martins, Woolworths, Tesco, Asda, Safeway and other paperback stockists.
Also available from Mills & Boon Reader Service, FREEPOST, PO Box 236, Croydon, Surrey CR9 9EL (UK Postage & Packing free).

MILLS & BOON

HEARTS OF FIRE by Miranda Lee

Welcome to our compelling family saga set in the glamorous world of opal dealing in Australia. Laden with dark secrets, forbidden desires and scandalous discoveries, **Hearts of Fire** unfolds over a series of 6 books, but each book also features a passionate romance with a happy ending and can be read independently.

Book 1: SEDUCTION & SACRIFICE
Published: April 1994   *FREE* with Book 2

WATCH OUT for special promotions!

Lenore had loved Zachary Marsden secretly for years. Loyal, handsome and protective, Zachary was the perfect husband. Only Zachary would never leave his wife...would he?

Book 2: DESIRE & DECEPTION
Published: April 1994   Price £2.50

Jade had a name for Kyle Armstrong: *Mr Cool*. He was the new marketing manager at Whitmore Opals—the job *she* coveted. However, the more she tried to hate this usurper, the more she found him attractive...

Book 3: PASSION & THE PAST
Published: May 1994   Price £2.50

Melanie was intensely attracted to Royce Grantham—which shocked her! She'd been so sure after the tragic end of her marriage that she would never feel for any man again. How strong was her resolve not to repeat past mistakes?

MILLS & BOON

HEARTS OF FIRE by Miranda Lee

Book 4: FANTASIES & THE FUTURE
Published: June 1994   Price £2.50

The man who came to mow the lawns was more stunning than any of Ava's fantasies, though she realised that Vincent Morelli thought she was just another rich, lonely housewife looking for excitement! But, Ava knew that her narrow, boring existence was gone forever...

Book 5: SCANDALS & SECRETS
Published: July 1994   Price £2.50

Celeste Campbell had lived on her hatred of Byron Whitmore for twenty years. Revenge was sweet...until news reached her that Byron was considering remarriage. Suddenly she found she could no longer deny all those long-buried feelings for him...

Book 6: MARRIAGE & MIRACLES
Published: August 1994   Price £2.50

Gemma's relationship with Nathan was in tatters, but her love for him remained intact—she was going to win him back! Gemma knew that Nathan's terrible past had turned his heart to stone, and she was asking for a miracle. But it was possible that one could happen, wasn't it?

Don't miss all six books!

Available from WH Smith, John Menzies, Volume One, Forbuoys, Martins, Woolworths, Tesco, Asda, Safeway and other paperback stockists. Also available from Mills & Boon Reader Service, FREEPOST, PO Box 236, Croydon, Surrey CR9 9EL (UK Postage & Packing free).

Next Month's Romances

Each month you can choose from a wide variety of romance with Mills & Boon. Below are the new titles to look out for next month, why not ask either Mills & Boon Reader Service or your Newsagent to reserve you a copy of the titles you want to buy – just tick the titles you would like and either post to Reader Service or take it to any Newsagent and ask them to order your books.

Please save me the following titles: — Please tick ✓

Title	Author	
PASSIONATE OPPONENT	Jenny Cartwright	
AN IMPOSSIBLE DREAM	Emma Darcy	
SHATTERED WEDDING	Elizabeth Duke	
A STRANGER'S KISS	Liz Fielding	
THE FURY OF LOVE	Natalie Fox	
THE LAST ILLUSION	Diana Hamilton	
DANGEROUS DESIRE	Sarah Holland	
STEPHANIE	Debbie Macomber	
BITTER MEMORIES	Margaret Mayo	
A TASTE OF PASSION	Kristy McCallum	
PHANTOM LOVER	Susan Napier	
WEDDING BELLS FOR BEATRICE	Betty Neels	
DARK VICTORY	Elizabeth Oldfield	
LOVE'S STING	Catherine Spencer	
CHASE A DREAM	Jennifer Taylor	
EDGE OF DANGER	Patricia Wilson	

If you would like to order these books in addition to your regular subscription from Mills & Boon Reader Service please send £1.90 per title to: Mills & Boon Reader Service, Freepost, P.O. Box 236, Croydon, Surrey, CR9 9EL, quote your Subscriber No:................................ (if applicable) and complete the name and address details below. Alternatively, these books are available from many local Newsagents including W H Smith, J Menzies, Martins and other paperback stockists from 8 July 1994.

Name:..
Address:...
....Post Code:..........................

To Retailer: If you would like to stock M&B books please contact your regular book/magazine wholesaler for details.

You may be mailed with offers from other reputable companies as a result of this application. If you would rather not take advantage of these opportunities please tick box. ☐

SUMMER SPECIAL!

Four exciting new Romances for the price of three

Each Romance features British heroines and their encounters with dark and desirable Mediterranean men. *Plus, a free Elmlea recipe booklet inside every pack.*

So sit back and enjoy your sumptuous summer reading pack and indulge yourself with the free Elmlea recipe ideas.

Available July 1994   Price £5.70

Available from WH Smith, John Menzies, Volume One, Forbuoys, Martins, Woolworths, Tesco, Asda, Safeway and other paperback stockists. Also available from Mills & Boon Reader Service, FREEPOST, PO Box 236, Croydon, Surrey CR9 9EL. (UK Postage & Packing free)

Accept 4 FREE Romances and 2 FREE gifts

FROM READER SERVICE

Here's an irresistible invitation from Mills & Boon. Please accept our offer of 4 FREE Romances, a CUDDLY TEDDY and a special MYSTERY GIFT! Then, if you choose, go on to enjoy 6 captivating Romances every month for just £1.90 each, postage and packing FREE. Plus our FREE Newsletter with author news, competitions and much more.

**Send the coupon below to:
Mills & Boon Reader Service,
FREEPOST, PO Box 236,
Croydon, Surrey CR9 9EL.**

NO STAMP REQUIRED

Yes! Please rush me 4 FREE Romances and 2 FREE gifts! Please also reserve me a Reader Service subscription. If I decide to subscribe I can look forward to receiving 6 brand new Romances for just £11.40 each month, post and packing FREE. If I decide not to subscribe I shall write to you within 10 days - I can keep the free books and gifts whatever I choose. I may cancel or suspend my subscription at any time. I am over 18 years of age.

Ms/Mrs/Miss/Mr _____ EP70R

Address _____

Postcode _____ Signature _____

Offer closes 31st October 1994. The right is reserved to refuse an application and change the terms of this offer. One application per household. Offer not valid for current subscribers to this series. Valid in UK and Eire only. Overseas readers please write for details. Southern Africa write to IBS Private Bag X3010, Randburg 2125. You may be mailed with offers from other reputable companies as a result of this application. Please tick box if you would prefer not to receive such offers ☐